| Freedom of the Press

Other books in the Issues on Trial series:

Freedom of the Press

Rob Edelman, Book Editor

GREENHAVEN PRESS

An imprint of Thomson Gale, a part of The Thomson Corporation

Detroit • New York • San Francisco • New Haven, Conn. • Waterville, Maine • London • Munich

Bonnie Szumski, *Publisher*
Helen Cothran, *Managing Editor*
Scott Barbour, *Series Editor*

© 2006 Thomson Gale, a part of The Thomson Corporation.

Thomson and Star logo are trademarks and Gale and Greenhaven Press are registered trademarks used herein under license.

For more information, contact:
Greenhaven Press
27500 Drake Rd.
Farmington Hills, MI 48331-3535
Or you can visit our Internet site at http://www.gale.com

LIBRARY OF CONGRESS CATALOGING-IN-PUBLICATION DATA

Freedom of the press / Rob Edelman, book editor.
    p. cm. -- (Issues on trial)
  Includes bibliographical references and index.
  0-7377-3449-3 (lib. : alk. paper)
  1. Freedom of the press--United States--Cases. I. Edelman, Rob. II. Series.
  KF4774.A7F74 2007
  342.7308'53--dc22
                                                    2006041173

Printed in the United States of America
10 9 8 7 6 5 4 3 2 1

Contents

Chapter 2: Protecting the Press Against Charges of Libel

Chapter 3: Balancing Press Freedom and National Security

Chapter 4: Requiring Reporters to Divulge Their Sources

Foreword

The U.S. courts have long served as a battleground for the most highly charged and contentious issues of the time. Divisive matters are often brought into the legal system by activists who feel strongly for their cause and demand an official resolution. Indeed, subjects that give rise to intense emotions or involve closely held religious or moral beliefs lay at the heart of the most polemical court rulings in history. One such case was *Brown v. Board of Education* (1954), which ended racial segregation in schools. Prior to *Brown*, the courts had held that blacks could be forced to use separate facilities as long as these facilities were equal to that of whites.

For years many groups had opposed segregation based on religious, moral, and legal grounds. Educators produced heartfelt testimony that segregated schooling greatly disadvantaged black children. They noted that in comparison to whites, blacks received a substandard education in deplorable conditions. Religious leaders such as Martin Luther King Jr. preached that the harsh treatment of blacks was immoral and unjust. Many involved in civil rights law, such as Thurgood Marshall, called for equal protection of all people under the law, as their study of the Constitution had indicated that segregation was illegal and un-American. Whatever their motivation for ending the practice, and despite the threats they received from segregationists, these ardent activists remained unwavering in their cause.

Those fighting against the integration of schools were mainly white southerners who did not believe that whites and blacks should intermingle. Blacks were subordinate to whites, they maintained, and society had to resist any attempt to break down strict color lines. Some white southerners charged that segregated schooling was *not* hindering blacks' education. For example, Virginia attorney general J. Lindsay Almond asserted, "With the help and the sympathy and the love and re-spect of the white people of the South, the colored man has risen under that educational process to a place of eminence and respect throughout the nation. It has served him well." So when the Supreme Court ruled against the segregationists in *Brown*, the South responded with vociferous cries of protest. Even government leaders criticized the decision. The governor of Arkansas, Orval Faubus, stated that he would not "be a party to any attempt to force acceptance of change to which the people are so overwhelmingly opposed." Indeed, resistance to integration was so great that when black students arrived at the formerly all-white Central High School in Arkansas, federal troops had to be dispatched to quell a threatening mob of protesters.

Nevertheless, the *Brown* decision was enforced and the South integrated its schools. In this instance, the Court, while not settling the issue to everyone's satisfaction, functioned as an instrument of progress by forcing a major social change. Historian David Halberstam observes that the *Brown* ruling "deprived segregationist practices of their moral legitimacy. . . . It was therefore perhaps the single most important moment of the decade, the moment that separated the old order from the new and helped create the tumultuous era just arriving." Considered one of the most important victories for civil rights, *Brown* paved the way for challenges to racial segregation in many areas, including on public buses and in restaurants.

In examining *Brown*, it becomes apparent that the courts play an influential role—and face an arduous challenge—in shaping the debate over emotionally charged social issues. Judges must balance competing interests, keeping in mind the high stakes and intense emotions on both sides. As exemplified by *Brown*, judicial decisions often upset the status quo and initiate significant changes in society. Greenhaven Press's Issues on Trial series captures the controversy surrounding influential court rulings and explores the social ramifications of such decisions from varying perspectives. Each anthology highlights one social issue—such as the death penalty, students' rights, or wartime civil liberties. Each volume then focuses on key historical and contemporary court cases that helped mold the issue as we know it today. The books include a compendium of primary sources—court rulings, dissents, and immediate reactions to the rulings—as well as secondary sources from experts in the field, people involved in the cases, legal analysts, and other commentators opining on the implications and legacy of the chosen cases. An annotated table of contents, an in-depth introduction, and prefaces that overview each case all provide context as readers delve into the topic at hand. To help students fully probe the subject, each volume contains book and periodical bibliographies, a comprehensive index, and a list of organizations to contact. With these features, the Issues on Trial series offers a well-rounded perspective on the courts' role in framing society's thorniest, most impassioned debates.

Introduction

A free press is one of the bulwarks of American democracy. The U.S. Constitution defines the three branches of government—legislative, executive, and judicial—and establishes the system of checks and balances to guarantee that one branch never can usurp power over the others. A free press, by monitoring the government and informing the public of its actions, essentially functions as the fourth branch of government. The founders of the nation were so mindful of the importance of the role of the press in a democratic society that they enshrined the right to a free press in the First Amendment.

Across the decades, the U.S. Supreme Court has played a crucial role in interpreting the First Amendment's freedom of the press provision. However, while the Court has repeatedly upheld the right, its rulings have not always been consistent. More often than not, the Supreme Court justices have disagreed on how far the right of a free press should extend.

In general, the Court's rulings have supported the right of the press—and those who concur with these decisions maintain that they reflect the spirit of the First Amendment. Such is the situation in three of the cases discussed in this book. In *Near v. Minnesota* (1931), the Court, in a five-to-four decision, determined that a state court cannot halt publication of a periodical based on the content of the articles it prints. In *New York Times v. Sullivan* (1964), the Court unanimously decreed that a journalist cannot be found guilty of libel for criticizing government officials unless the officials prove that the statements the journalist made about them were purposefully malicious. In *New York Times Company v. United States* (1971), more commonly known as the Pentagon Papers case, the

Court ruled in a six-to-three decision that journalists may freely uncover and report facts about government impropriety.

In each of these three instances, the Court backed up the free press provision by stating that the media have the right to publish material that some—including politicians and other powerful people—may find objectionable. For example, *New York Times Company v. United States* centered on the efforts of the administration of President Richard Nixon to prevent the *New York Times* and *Washington Post* from publishing the Pentagon Papers, a seven-thousand-page classified report tracing the evolution of America's Vietnam War policy from 1945 to 1968. The report cited instances of miscommunication and secrecy between the branches of the federal government and falsehoods imparted to the American people by government representatives—including former presidents. The Court ruled that, while publication of the Pentagon Papers might embarrass the offending officials, it would neither impair the nation's security nor imperil the safety of American soldiers fighting in Vietnam. In his opinion in the case, Justice Hugo L. Black cited the important role a free press plays in guarding against government misconduct: "In the First Amendment, the Founding Fathers gave the free press the protection it must have to fulfill its essential role in our democracy. The press was to serve the governed, not the governors. . . . Only a free and unrestrained press can effectively expose deception in government."[1]

Press freedom does not extend only to criticism of public officials and policies. In order to ensure that the United States remains an open society, the Court routinely has found it necessary to allow speech that is offensive to the majority or that some individuals may find objectionable. In *Near v. Minnesota*, the Court struck down a Minnesota state law that permitted judges to halt the publication of periodicals they considered "obscene, lewd, and lascivious" or "malicious, scandalous, and defamatory." The case centered on the *Saturday Press*, a scandal sheet whose publisher, J.M. (Jay) Near, was notorious for being antilabor, antiblack, anti-Catholic, and anti-Semitic. The Court's rationale for this and similar rulings was that, in order to ensure that information flows in a democracy freely, it is necessary to allow journalists the greatest latitude possible to report their stories. The offending speech that occasionally may result is simply the price society pays for true democracy. In his opinion in *Near v. Minnesota*, Charles Evans Hughes quoted James Madison, who stated the point memorably: "Some degree of abuse is inseparable from the proper use of everything, and in no instance is this more true than in that of the press. It has accordingly been decided by the practice of the States that it is better to leave a few of its noxious branches to their luxuriant growth than, by pruning them away, to injure the vigour of those yielding the proper fruits."[2]

While the Court ruled in favor of the press in *Near v. Minnesota, New York Times Company v. United States*, and *New York Times v. Sullivan*, it is essential to emphasize that two of the decisions were not unanimous. In each, minority opinions favored press restrictions. In *Near v. Minnesota*, Pierce Butler, one of the dissenting justices, declared that the government had a right to rein in the press when it abused its right: "In this case, there was previous publication made in the course of the business of regularly producing malicious, scandalous and defamatory periodicals. . . . The business and publications unquestionably constitute an abuse of the right of free press. . . . There is no question of the power of the State to denounce such transgressions."[3]

Similarly, in his dissenting opinion in *New York Times Company v. United States*, John Marshall Harlan II insisted that the courts should defer to the executive branch in determining whether publication of certain materials would cause a breach of national security. He quoted John Marshall, the

Court's chief justice from 1801 to 1835: "The President is the sole organ of the nation in its external relations, and its sole representative with foreign nations."[4] Thus, if the president declares that the dissemination of certain material would cause a breach of national security, the courts should uphold the government's restraint of the press.

In *Branzburg v. Hayes* (1972), the fourth case examined in this book, the majority ruling was perceived as a blow to press freedom. The Court determined that, when summoned by grand juries, journalists are obliged to reveal the identities of people who have provided them with information for their stories on a confidential basis. Reporters object to this requirement because they claim it hampers the gathering of facts; potential sources of information will be less willing to cooperate with journalists if they know their identities may later be made public. Therefore, news professionals believe they should be granted immunity from the requirement to divulge their sources. In *Branzburg*, Justice Byron R. White rejected the argument that the requirement to name sources harmed the press: "This conclusion itself involves no restraint on what newspapers may publish or on the type or quality of information reporters may seek to acquire, nor does it threaten the vast bulk of confidential relationships between reporters and their sources."[5]

As in *Near v. Minnesota* and *New York Times Company v. United States*, the Court in *Branzburg* was not unanimous. In his dissenting judgment in *Branzburg*, William O. Douglas declared that the First Amendment does in fact shield journalists from the requirement to testify before grand juries and divulge their sources. He argued that requiring journalists to provide such information would indeed hamper the ability of the press to perform its crucial function: "A reporter is no better than his source of information. Unless he has a privilege to withhold the identity of his source, he will be the victim of governmental intrigue or aggression. If he can be summoned to testify in secret before a grand jury, his sources will dry up and the attempted exposure, the effort to enlighten the public, will be ended."[6]

As these examples reveal, Supreme Court justices have been far from unanimous on the proper limits of press freedom. However, in most instances the Court has approached the First Amendment with the reverence it deserves, upholding and expanding the right of the press to remain free from prior restraint and frivolous charges of libel. Thus equipped with the free press clause of the First Amendment, the press continues to perform its role as a guardian of American democracy.

Notes

1. Hugo L. Black, *New York Times Company v. United States*, majority opinion, 1971.
2. Charles Evans Hughes, *Near v. Minnesota*, majority opinion, 1931.
3. Pierce Butler, *Near v. Minnesota*, dissenting opinion, 1931.
4. John Marshall Harlan II, *New York Times Company v. United States*, dissenting opinion, 1971.
5. Byron R. White, *Branzburg v. Hayes*, majority opinion, 1972.
6. William O. Douglas, *Branzburg v. Hayes*, dissenting opinion, 1972.

CHAPTER 1

Declaring Prior Restraint Unconstitutional

Chapter Preface

Case Overview: *Near v. Minnesota (1931)* In 1925 the Minnesota State Legislature passed the Public Nuisance Abatement Law. This legislation allowed individuals to file lawsuits against—and judges to halt publication of—any periodical that printed material they deemed "obscene, lewd, and lascivious" or "malicious, scandalous, and defamatory." Those who opposed the legislation labeled it the "Minnesota Gag Law."

Two years later the law was applied to the *Saturday Press*, a Minneapolis-based weekly newspaper published by J.M. (Jay) Near. Near was a controversial figure, who was recognized for being antilabor, antiblack, anti-Catholic, and anti-Semitic. His paper was a scandal sheet. For example, on November 19, 1927, the *Saturday Press* ran an editorial that asserted, "There have been too many men in this city and especially those in official life, who HAVE been taking orders and suggestions from JEW GANGSTERS, therefore we HAVE Jew Gangsters, practically ruling Minneapolis." The editorial went on to claim, "It is Jew thugs who have 'pulled' practically every robbery in this city."

Hennepin County attorney Floyd B. Olson, who frequently was attacked in the *Saturday Press*, employed the Public Nuisance Abatement Law in an attempt to close down the paper. With the support of Colonel Robert R. McCormick, influential publisher of the *Chicago Tribune*, Near battled the authorities over the suppression of the *Saturday Press*. The Minnesota State Supreme Court, however, upheld the law, decreeing that "press (freedom) does not mean that an evil-minded person may publish just anything."

The case eventually reached the U.S. Supreme Court. On June 1, 1931, in a 5–4 decision, the Court determined that the Minnesota law was unconstitutional, ruling that it stifled the First Amendment's free press guarantees and the Fourteenth

Amendment's clause affirming that no state shall deprive any citizen of life, liberty, or property without due process of law. The state law was a case of "prior restraint," meaning that it banned issues of the *Saturday Press* before they were published. According to the ruling, a court cannot halt publication of a periodical based on the type of articles it prints. A court can determine if the articles are libelous or injurious only after they have been printed and disseminated. The Supreme Court ruling allowed the *Saturday Press* to resume publication.

Near v. Minnesota was a landmark Supreme Court ruling. It was the first important Court decision involving freedom of the press; for the first time, the Court decreed that a state law was unconstitutional if it impinged on the freedom of speech and press guaranteed by the First Amendment. Previously, the Court had interpreted the First Amendment as limiting only the actions of the Federal government. Furthermore, the decision allowed journalists to avoid being censored by elected officials and their representatives.

Near v. Minnesota impacted several subsequent high-profile cases. For example, it was cited in *New York Times v. Sullivan* (1964), which made it difficult for public officials to stifle press freedom by filing libel suits, and *New York Times Company v. United States* (1971), which allowed the *New York Times*, *Washington Post*, and other newspapers to publish the Pentagon Papers, classified government documents relating to the genesis of the Vietnam War.

> *"The fact that the liberty of the press may be abused by miscreant purveyors of scandal does not make any the less necessary the immunity of the press from previous restraint."*

The Court's Decision: Prior Restraint Is Unconstitutional

Charles Evans Hughes

In Near v. Minnesota *the U.S. Supreme Court ruled that a Minnesota statute banning the publication of the weekly* Saturday Press *was unconstitutional despite the abrasive nature of the paper's content. In this excerpt from his majority opinion, Charles Evans Hughes writes that the law is unconstitutional because it stifles freedom of the press. On occasion, publishing certain information is inappropriate. For example, if the nation is at war, it is in the nation's interest to prevent a newspaper from printing data related to troop movements. However, according to Hughes, no such national interest was at stake in the case of* Near v. Minnesota. *Therefore, shutting down the paper was an unconstitutional form of prior restraint.*

Hughes, a native New Yorker, served as New York governor and U.S. secretary of state and was the Republican Party presidential nominee in 1916. He was a Supreme Court justice from 1910 to 1916 and was appointed chief justice in 1930. He retired in 1941 and died seven years later.

This [Minnesota] statute, for the suppression as a public nuisance of a newspaper or periodical, is unusual, if not unique, and raises questions of grave importance transcending

Charles Evans Hughes, majority opinion, *Near v. Minnesota*, 1931.

the local interests involved in the particular action. It is no longer open to doubt that the liberty of the press, and of speech, is within the liberty safeguarded by the due process clause of the Fourteenth Amendment from invasion by state action. It was found impossible to conclude that this essential personal liberty of the citizen was left unprotected by the general guaranty of fundamental rights of person and property. In maintaining this guaranty, the authority of the State to enact laws to promote the health, safety, morals and general welfare of its people is necessarily admitted. The limits of this sovereign power must always be determined with appropriate regard to the particular subject of its exercise. . . . Liberty of speech, and of the press, is . . . not an absolute right, and the State may punish its abuse. Liberty, in each of its phases, has its history and connotation, and, in the present instance, the inquiry is as to the historic conception of the liberty of the press and whether the statute under review violates the essential attributes of that liberty. . . .

The Meaning of the Statute

The operation and effect of the statute, in substance, is that public authorities may bring the owner or publisher of a newspaper or periodical before a judge upon a charge of conducting a business of publishing scandalous and defamatory matter—in particular, that the matter consists of charges against public officers of official dereliction—and, unless the owner or publisher is able and disposed to bring competent evidence to satisfy the judge that the charges are true and are published with good motives and for justifiable ends, his newspaper or periodical is suppressed and further publication is made punishable as a contempt. This is of the essence of censorship.

The question is whether a statute authorizing such proceedings in restraint of publication is consistent with the conception of the liberty of the press as historically conceived and guaranteed. In determining the extent of the constitutional protection, it has been generally, if not universally, considered that it is the chief purpose of the guaranty to prevent previous restraints upon publication. The struggle in England, directed against the legislative power of the licenser [official censor], resulted in renunciation of the censorship of the press. The liberty deemed to be established was thus described by [eighteenth-century legal scholar Sir William] Blackstone:

> The liberty of the press is indeed essential to the nature of a free state; but this consists in laying no *previous* restraints upon publications, and not in freedom from censure for criminal matter when published. Every freeman has an undoubted right to lay what sentiments he pleases before the public; to forbid this is to destroy the freedom of the press; but if he publishes what is improper, mischievous or illegal, he must take the consequence of his own temerity.

Freedom from Executive and Legislative Restraint

The distinction was early pointed out between the extent of the freedom with respect to censorship under our constitutional system and that enjoyed in England. Here, as [Founding Father James] Madison said,

> the great and essential rights of the people are secured against legislative as well as against executive ambition. They are secured not by laws paramount to prerogative, but by constitutions paramount to laws. This security of the freedom of the press requires that it should be exempt not only from previous restraint by the Executive, as in Great Britain, but from legislative restraint also.

This Court said, in *Patterson v. Colorado* [1907]:

> In the first place, the main purpose of such constitutional provisions is "to prevent all such previous restraints upon publications as had been practiced by other governments,"

and they do not prevent the subsequent punishment of such as may be deemed contrary to the public welfare. The preliminary freedom extends as well to the false as to the true; the subsequent punishment may extend as well to the true as to the false. This was the law of criminal libel apart from statute in most cases, if not in all. . . .

Libel Laws Protect from Press Abuse

But it is recognized that punishment for the abuse of the liberty accorded to the press is essential to the protection of the public, and that the common law rules that subject the libeler to responsibility for the public offense, as well as for the private injury, are not abolished by the protection extended in our constitutions. The law of criminal libel rests upon that secure foundation. There is also the conceded authority of courts to punish for contempt when publications directly tend to prevent the proper discharge of judicial functions. In the present case, we have no occasion to inquire as to the permissible scope of subsequent punishment. For whatever wrong the appellant has committed or may commit by his publications the State appropriately affords both public and private redress by its libel laws. . . . The statute in question does not deal with punishments; it provides for no punishment, except in case of contempt for violation of the court's order, but for suppression and injunction, that is, for restraint upon publication.

Prior Restraint Is Allowed in Exceptional Cases

The objection has also been made that the principle as to immunity from previous restraint is stated too broadly, if every such restraint is deemed to be prohibited. That is undoubtedly true; the protection even as to previous restraint is not absolutely unlimited. But the limitation has been recognized only in exceptional cases:

> When a nation is at war, many things that might be said in time of peace are such a hindrance to its effort that their utterance will not be endured so long as men fight, and that no Court could regard them as protected by any constitutional right. [*Schenck v. United States* (1919).]

No one would question but that a government might prevent actual obstruction to its recruiting service or the publication of the sailing dates of transports or the number and location of troops. On similar grounds, the primary requirements of decency may be enforced against obscene publications. The security of the community life may be protected against incitements to acts of violence and the overthrow by force of orderly government. The constitutional guaranty of free speech does not

> protect a man from an injunction against uttering words that may have all the effect of force. [*Gompers v. Buck Stove & Range Co.* [1911].]

These limitations are not applicable here. Nor are we now concerned with questions as to the extent of authority to prevent publications in order to protect private rights according to the principles governing the exercise of the jurisdiction of courts of equity.

The Press and Censorship

The exceptional nature of its limitations places in a strong light the general conception that liberty of the press, historically considered and taken up by the Federal Constitution, has meant, principally, although not exclusively, immunity from previous restraints or censorship. The conception of the liberty of the press in this country had broadened with the exigencies of the colonial period and with the efforts to secure freedom from oppressive administration. That liberty was especially cherished for the immunity it afforded from previous restraint of the publication of censure of public officers and charges of official misconduct. As was said by [Massachusetts Supreme Judicial Court] Chief Justice [Isaac] Parker, in *Commonwealth v. Blanding* [1825], with respect to the constitution of Massachusetts:

> Besides, it is well understood, and received as a commentary on this provision for the liberty of the press, that it was intended to prevent all such *previous restraints* upon publications as had been practiced by other governments, and in early times here, to stifle the efforts of patriots towards enlightening their fellow subjects upon their rights and the duties of rulers. The liberty of the press was to be unrestrained, but he who used it was to be responsible in case of its abuse.

In the letter sent by the Continental Congress (October 26, 1774) to the Inhabitants of Quebec, referring to the "five great rights," it was said:

> The last right we shall mention regards the freedom of the press. The importance of this consists, besides the advancement of truth, science, morality, and arts in general, in its diffusion of liberal sentiments on the administration of Government, its ready communication of thoughts between subjects, and its consequential promotion of union among them whereby oppressive officers are shamed or intimidated into more honourable and just modes of conducting affairs.

Free Press Guaranties in State Constitutions

Madison, who was the leading spirit in the preparation of the First Amendment of the Federal Constitution, thus described the practice and sentiment which led to the guaranties of liberty of the press in state constitutions:

> In every State, probably, in the Union, the press has exerted a freedom in canvassing the merits and measures of public men of every description which has not been confined to the strict limits of the common law. On this footing the

freedom of the press has stood; on this footing it yet stands.
. . . Some degree of abuse is inseparable from the proper use
of everything, and in no instance is this more true than in
that of the press. It has accordingly been decided by the
practice of the States that it is better to leave a few of its
noxious branches to their luxuriant growth than, by pruning
them away, to injure the vigour of those yielding the proper
fruits. . . .

The fact that, for approximately one hundred and fifty
years, there has been almost an entire absence of attempts to
impose previous restraints upon publications relating to the
malfeasance of public officers is significant of the deep-seated
conviction that such restraints would violate constitutional
right. Public officers, whose character and conduct remain
open to debate and free discussion in the press, find their
remedies for false accusations in actions under libel laws providing for redress and punishment, and not in proceedings to
restrain the publication of newspapers and periodicals. The
general principle that the constitutional guaranty of the liberty of the press gives immunity from previous restraints has
been approved in many decisions under the provisions of
state constitutions.

The importance of this immunity has not lessened. While
reckless assaults upon public men, and efforts to bring oblo-
quy upon those who are endeavoring faithfully to discharge
official duties, exert a baleful influence and deserve the sever-
est condemnation in public opinion, it cannot be said that
this abuse is greater, and it is believed to be less, than that
which characterized the period in which our institutions took
shape. Meanwhile, the administration of government has become more complex, the opportunities for malfeasance and
corruption have multiplied, crime has grown to most serious
proportions, and the danger of its protection by unfaithful officials and of the impairment of the fundamental security of
life and property by criminal alliances and official neglect, em-

phasizes the primary need of a vigilant and courageous press, especially in great cities. The fact that the liberty of the press may be abused by miscreant purveyors of scandal does not make any the less necessary the immunity of the press from previous restraint in dealing with official misconduct. Subsequent punishment for such abuses as may exist is the appropriate remedy consistent with constitutional privilege. . . .

The Statute Cannot Be Defended

The statute in question cannot be justified by reason of the fact that the publisher is permitted to show, before injunction issues, that the matter published is true and is published with good motives and for justifiable ends. If such a statute, authorizing suppression and injunction on such a basis, is constitutionally valid, it would be equally permissible for the legislature to provide that at any time the publisher of any newspaper could be brought before a court, or even an administrative officer . . . and required to produce proof of the truth of his publication, or of what he intended to publish, and of his motives, or stand enjoined. If this can be done, the legislature may provide machinery for determining in the complete exercise of its discretion what are justifiable ends, and restrain publication accordingly. And it would be but a step to a complete system of censorship. . . .

Equally unavailing is the insistence that the statute is designed to prevent the circulation of scandal which tends to disturb the public peace and to provoke assaults and the commission of crime. Charges of reprehensible conduct, and in particular of official malfeasance, unquestionably create a public scandal, but the theory of the constitutional guaranty is that even a more serious public evil would be caused by authority to prevent publication. . . .

There is nothing new in the fact that charges of reprehensible conduct may create resentment and the disposition to resort to violent means of redress, but this well understood tendency did not alter the determination to protect the press against censorship and restraint upon publication. As was said in *New Yorker Staats-Zeitung v. Nolan*:

> If the township may prevent the circulation of a newspaper for no reason other than that some of its inhabitants may violently disagree with it, and resent its circulation by resorting to physical violence, there is no limit to what may be prohibited.

The danger of violent reactions becomes greater with effective organization of defiant groups resenting exposure, and if this consideration warranted legislative interference with the initial freedom of publication, the constitutional protection would be reduced to a mere form of words.

For these reasons we hold the statute . . . to be an infringement of the liberty of the press guaranteed by the Fourteenth Amendment. We should add that this decision rests upon the operation and effect of the statute, without regard to the question of the truth of the charges contained in the particular periodical. The fact that the public officers named in this case, and those associated with the charges of official dereliction, may be deemed to be impeccable cannot affect the conclusion that the statute imposes an unconstitutional restraint upon publication.

"It is of the greatest importance that the States shall be . . . free to employ all just and appropriate measures to prevent abuses of the liberty of the press."

Dissenting Opinion: Freedom of the Press Has Limits

Pierce Butler

Four U.S. Supreme Court justices—Pierce Butler, James Clark McReynolds, Willis Van Devanter, and George Sutherland—dissented from the majority opinion in Near v. Minnesota. *The case involved a Minnesota statute that allowed officials to ban the publication of newspapers or magazines that previously had printed material deemed by a judge to be "malicious" or "lascivious." In this excerpt from his dissenting opinion, Butler maintains that scandal sheets like the* Saturday Press, *the newspaper at the center of the case, exploit the right to freedom of the press. States should be allowed by law to denounce such publications and ban them. Furthermore, prior restraint does not pertain because officials are not preventing the publication of specific content. Rather, such laws merely are nuisance abatement measures.*

Butler, a Minnesotan and staunch conservative, was appointed to the Supreme Court in 1923. He remained on the bench until his death in 1939.

The decision of the Court in this case declares Minnesota and every other State powerless to restrain by injunction the business of publishing and circulating among the people malicious, scandalous and defamatory periodicals that in due

Pierce Butler, dissenting opinion, *Near v. Minnesota*, 1931.

course of judicial procedure has been adjudged to be a public nuisance. It gives to freedom of the press a meaning and a scope not heretofore recognized, and construes "liberty" in the due process clause of the Fourteenth Amendment to put upon the States a federal restriction that is without precedent.

Confessedly, the Federal Constitution, prior to 1868, when the Fourteenth Amendment was adopted, did not protect the right of free speech or press against state action. Up to that time, the right was safeguarded solely by the constitutions and laws of the States, and, it may be added, they operated adequately to protect it. This Court was not called on until 1925 to decide whether the "liberty" protected by the Fourteenth Amendment includes the right of free speech and press. That question has been finally answered in the affirmative.

Publishing False and Malicious Articles

The record shows, and it is conceded, that defendants' [J.M. Near's] regular business was the publication of malicious, scandalous and defamatory articles concerning the principal public officers, leading newspapers of the city, many private persons and the Jewish race. It also shows that it was their purpose at all hazards to continue to carry on the business. In every edition, slanderous and defamatory matter predominates to the practical exclusion of all else. Many of the statements are so highly improbable as to compel a finding that they are false. The articles themselves show malice.

The defendant here has no standing to assert that the statute is invalid because it might be construed so as to violate the Constitution. His right is limited solely to the inquiry whether, having regard to the points properly raised in his case, the effect of applying the statute is to deprive him of his liberty without due process of law. This Court should not reverse the judgment below [Minnesota State Supreme Court judgment] upon the ground that, in some other case, the statute may be applied in a way that is repugnant to the freedom of the press protected by the Fourteenth Amendment. . . .

Near's Rationale

Defendant concedes that the editions of the newspaper complained of are "defamatory *per se*," and he says:

> It has been asserted that the constitution was never intended to be a shield for malice, scandal, and defamation when untrue, or published with bad motives, or for unjustifiable ends. . . . The contrary is true; every person *does* have a constitutional right to publish malicious, scandalous, and defamatory matter though untrue, and with bad motives, and for unjustifiable ends, *in the first instance*, though he is subject to responsibility therefor *afterwards*.

The record, when the substance of the articles is regarded, requires that concession here. And this Court is required to pass on the validity of the state law on that basis. . . .

The Act was passed in the exertion of the State's power of police, and this court is, by well established rule, required to assume, until the contrary is clearly made to appear, that there exists in Minnesota a state of affairs that justifies this measure for the preservation of the peace and good order of the State.
. . .

It is of the greatest importance that the States shall be untrammeled and free to employ all just and appropriate measures to prevent abuses of the liberty of the press.

Press Freedom and Responsibility

In his work on the Constitution (5th ed.), Justice [Joseph] Story, expounding the First Amendment, which declares "Congress shall make no law abridging the freedom of speech or of the press," said:

> That this amendment was intended to secure to every citizen an absolute right to speak, or write, or print whatever

he might please, without any responsibility, public or private, therefore is a supposition too wild to be indulged by any rational man. This would be to allow to every citizen a right to destroy at his pleasure the reputation, the peace, the property, and even the personal safety of every other citizen. A man might, out of mere malice and revenge, accuse another of the most infamous crimes; might excite against him the indignation of all his fellow citizens by the most atrocious calumnies; might disturb, nay, overturn, all his domestic peace, and embitter his parental affections; might inflict the most distressing punishments upon the weak, the timid, and the innocent; might prejudice all a man's civil, and political, and private rights, and might stir up sedition, rebellion, and treason even against the government itself in the wantonness of his passions or the corruption of his heart. Civil society could not go on under such circumstances. Men would then be obliged to resort to private vengeance to make up for the deficiencies of the law, and assassination and savage cruelties would be perpetrated with all the frequency belonging to barbarous and brutal communities. It is plain, then, that the language of this amendment imports no more than that every man shall have a right to speak, write, and print his opinions upon any subject whatsoever, without any prior restraint, so always that he does not injure any other person in his rights, person, property, or reputation, and so always that he does not thereby disturb the public peace or attempt to subvert the government. It is neither more nor less than an expansion of the great doctrine recently brought into operation in the law of libel, *that every man shall be at liberty to publish what is true, with good motives and for justifiable ends.* And, with this reasonable limitation, it is not only right in itself, but it is an inestimable privilege in a free government. Without such a limitation, it might become the scourge of the republic, first denouncing the principles of liberty and then, by rendering the most virtuous patriots odious through the terrors of the press, introducing despotism in its worst form. (Italicizing added.)

The Historical Basis of the Ban
Against Prior Restraint

The Court quotes [eighteenth-century legal scholar William] Blackstone in support of its condemnation of the statute as imposing a previous restraint upon publication. But the previous restraints referred to by him subjected the press to the arbitrary will of an administrative officer. He describes the practice:

> To subject the press to the restrictive power of a licenser, as was formerly done both before and since the revolution [of 1688], is to subject all freedom of sentiment to the prejudices of one man and make him the arbitrary and infallible judge of all controverted points in learning, religion, and government.

Story gives the history alluded to by Blackstone:

> The art of printing soon after its introduction, we are told, was looked upon, as well in England as in other countries, as merely a matter of state, and subject to the coercion of the crown. It was, therefore, regulated in England by the king's proclamations, prohibitions, charters of privilege, and licenses, and finally by the degrees of the Court of Star-Chamber, which limited the number of printers and of presses which each should employ, and prohibited new publications unless previously approved by proper licensers. On the demolition of this odious jurisdiction, in 1641, the Long Parliament of Charles the First, after their rupture with that prince, assumed the same powers which the Star-Chamber exercised with respect to licensing books, and during the Commonwealth (such is human frailty and the love of power even in republics), they issued their ordinances for that purpose, founded principally upon a Star-Chamber decree of 1637. After the restoration of Charles the Second, a statute on the same subject was passed, copied, with some few alterations, from the parliamentary ordinances. The act expired in 1679, and was revived and continued for a few

years after the revolution of 1688. Many attempts were made by the government to keep it in force, but it was so strongly resisted by Parliament that it expired in 1694, and has never since been revived.

It is plain that Blackstone taught that, under the common law liberty of the press means simply the absence of restraint upon publication in advance as distinguished from liability, civil or criminal, for libelous or improper matter so published. And, as above shown, Story defined freedom of the press guaranteed by the First Amendment to mean that "every man shall be at liberty to publish what is true, with good motives and for justifiable ends." His statement concerned the definite declaration of the First Amendment. It is not suggested that the freedom of press included in the liberty protected by the Fourteenth Amendment [i.e., against state action], which was adopted after Story's definition, is greater than that protected against congressional action.

Minnesota Statute Does Not Constitute Prior Restraint

The Minnesota statute does not operate as a *previous* restraint on publication within the proper meaning of that phrase. It does not authorize administrative control in advance such as was formerly exercised by the licensers and censors but prescribes a remedy to be enforced by a suit in equity. In this case, there was previous publication made in the course of the business of regularly producing malicious, scandalous and defamatory periodicals. The business and publications unquestionably constitute an abuse of the right of free press. The statute denounces the things done as a nuisance on the ground, as stated by the state supreme court, that they threaten morals, peace and good order. There is no question of the power of the State to denounce such transgressions. The restraint authorized is only in respect of continuing to do what has been duly adjudged to constitute a nuisance. The controlling words are

> All persons guilty of such nuisance may be enjoined, as hereinafter provided. . . . Whenever any such nuisance is committed . . . , an action in the name of the State

may be brought

> to perpetually enjoin the person or persons committing, conducting or maintaining any such nuisance, *from further committing, conducting or maintaining any such nuisance. . . .* The court may make its order and judgment permanently enjoining . . . defendants found guilty . . . from committing or continuing the acts prohibited hereby, and in and by such judgment, such nuisance may be wholly abated. . . .

There is nothing in the statute purporting to prohibit publications that have not been adjudged to constitute a nuisance. It is fanciful to suggest similarity between the granting or enforcement of the decree authorized by this statute to prevent *further* publication of malicious, scandalous and defamatory articles and the *previous* restraint upon the press by licensers as referred to by Blackstone and described in the history of the times to which he alludes. . . .

It is well known, as found by the state supreme court, that existing libel laws are inadequate effectively to suppress evils resulting from the kind of business and publications that are shown in this case. The doctrine that measures such as the one before us are invalid because they operate as previous restraints to infringe freedom of press exposes the peace and good order of every community and the business and private affairs of every individual to the constant and protracted false and malicious assaults of any insolvent publisher who may have purpose and sufficient capacity to contrive and put into effect a scheme or program for oppression, blackmail or extortion. The judgment should be affirmed.

> "Freedom of the press was transformed successfully from an eighteenth- and nineteenth-century ideal into a twentieth-century constitutional bulwark."

Near Was a Landmark Decision for Press Freedom

Fred W. Friendly

In Near v. Minnesota *(1931) the U.S. Supreme Court overturned a Minnesota state law that permitted judges to halt publication of periodicals they deemed "obscene" or "malicious." In this chapter from the book* Minnesota Rag, *written decades after* Near v. Minnesota *was handed down, Fred W. Friendly revisits the decision and examines its impact on the American media. The Supreme Court's ruling that the Minnesota law was unconstitutional solidified the First Amendment's free press guarantees, according to Friendly. It also impacted mightily on subsequent free-press cases that came before the Court, including* New York Times v. Sullivan *(1964) and* New York Times Company v. United States *(1971).*

Friendly, who died in 1998, was a pioneering CBS television news producer. In the 1950s he cocreated (with Edward R. Murrow) See It Now, *the landmark documentary television series. He also served as president of CBS News.*

Although his name is hardly a household word, the ghost of Jay M. Near still stalks most U.S. courtrooms. There exists no plaque that bears his name, and even [*Chicago Tribune* publisher] Colonel [Robert R.] McCormick's marble memorial to Chief Justice [Charles Evans] Hughes's opinion omits the name of the case. *Near* is truly the unknown soldier in the continuing struggle between the powers of government and the power of the press to publish the news.

Near v. Minnesota placed freedom of the press "in the least favorable light"; as Minnesota and New York newspapers and lawyers viewed the litigation, it was the worst possible case. But perhaps it is just because Near's cause did not at first appear to be significant, except to Colonel McCormick and [American Civil Liberties Union founder] Roger Baldwin, that it created such sturdy law. So indestructible has it proved that its storied progeny, the Pentagon Papers case, was able to survive the political firestorms of 1971. If "great cases like hard cases make bad law," as the [Oliver Wendell] Holmes proverb warns, it may follow that since few knew or cared about Near's cause, freedom of the press was transformed successfully from an eighteenth- and nineteenth-century ideal into a twentieth-century constitutional bulwark.

By his admonition, Holmes meant that volatile national confrontations which appeal to prejudices and distort judgment can be counterproductive in shaping the law of the future. Such emotional conflicts as slavery, as in the Dred Scott decision, and child-labor laws, as in *Adkins [v. Children's Hospital* (1923)]*, Holmes suggested . . . , "exercise a kind of hydraulic pressure which makes what previously was clear seem doubtful, and before which even well-settled principles of law will bend." In 1931 an American public plagued by economic panic, unemployment, Prohibition and the likes of [mobster] Al Capone cared little about the civil rights of a scandalmonger from Minnesota. To paraphrase Holmes, Near's case embodied all the underwhelming interests required to shape the grand law of the future. His success was based not in frenzied national debate, but in quirks-of-fate delays in the Minnesota courts, the deaths of two conservative Justices, and [President Herbert] Hoover's subsequent appointments. It was the new

Chief Justice who made the difference, not simply because he added one more vote to Near's side, but because of his unexpected passion for the First Amendment and his intellectual capacity to lead others, especially Justice [Owen] Roberts.

A Potent Guide

The precedent of *Near v. Minnesota* has withstood onslaughts from Presidents, legislatures and even the judiciary itself in its attempts to enforce basic rights which seemed to clash with the First Amendment. It demonstrated the latent strengths for an amendment which had gone untested for 150 years. That five-to-four decision achieved far more than simply asserting Near's rights. Like [free speech activist] Yetta Stromberg's case, announced two weeks earlier in 1931, it marked the beginning of a concerted process "to plug the holes punched in the Bill of Rights," and what [newspaperman/political commentator H.L.] Mencken had called in 1926 "the most noble opportunity that the Supreme Court, in all its history, ever faced."

Another gaping hole was repaired in 1937 when the Hughes court, with Benjamin N. Cardozo having replaced Holmes, established in *De Jonge v. Oregon* for free speech and assembly what *Near* had established for freedom of the press. The case involved syndicalism, a Portland streetcar conductor's right to attend a Communist meeting in a public hall. Again Hughes contributed the majority opinion: "The greater the importance of safeguarding the community from incitement . . . by force and violence, the more imperative is the need to preserve inviolate the constitutional rights of free speech, free press and free assembly . . . Therein lies the security of the Republic, the very foundation of constitutional government."

Impact on Future Cases

There have been hundreds of other press cases before the Court since 1931—some won, some lost. Perhaps the seminal judgment was the 1964 decision in *New York Times Co v. Sul-*

livan, which prevented Southern courts from using the law of libel to thwart national news coverage of the civil rights battle. Although not a prior-restraint case, *Sullivan* freed the press from the threat of chilling damages in reporting the conduct of public officials in Alabama in the explosive sixties. Associate Justice William Brennan's majority opinion established that officials, and later public figures, could not recover libel damages for reports concerning their official actions without proving "malice," that is, deliberate lying or "reckless disregard for the truth."

But *Near*'s ultimate legacy was finally realized forty years later, almost to the day, in the clash between the power of the presidency of the United States and two powerful newspapers, the *New York Times*, and the *Washington Post*. Its official name was *New York Times Co. v. United States*, but it is remembered as the Pentagon Papers case. It began when the *New York Times* obtained a forty-seven-volume secret history of the Vietnam war from Daniel Ellsberg, a former analyst of the Rand Corporation; it ended with a major victory for the press in the Supreme Court. On June 13, 1971, the *New York Times* began publishing its synopsis and analysis of the secret documents, and two days later the [Richard M.] Nixon Administration began legal efforts to restrain it. Later that week the government also sought to enjoin the *Washington Post* from publishing the same classified material. In a "frenzied train of events," as one Justice described it, the cases bobbed back and forth between district and appeals courts until, eleven days later, the Supreme Court agreed to try to untangle the conflicting and confusing opinions.

Citing *Near*

What dominated all the arguments in all briefs and opinions, from district court to Supreme Court, was the theory of no previous restraint, codified by [eighteenth-century English legal scholar Sir William] Blackstone and incorporated by ["Father of the U.S. Constitution" James] Madison, but made concrete in *Near*.

The Court met hastily on Saturday morning, June 25, and five days later announced its six-to-three decision. Leaning heavily on *Near v. Minnesota*, the Court held that the heavy burden of justifying the imposition of prior restraint had not been met by the government. It required nine opinions for the Supreme Court to explain its votes, and *Near* was cited ten times.

Justice William O. Douglas, in an opinion joined by Justice Hugo Black, quoted long passages from Chief Justice Hughes's majority opinion in *Near*. Believing that the government had no power to punish or restrain "material that is embarrassing to the powers-that-be," Douglas and Black reiterated Hughes's opinion: "The fact that liberty of the press may be abused . . . does not make any less necessary the immunity of the press." But it was Douglas' concluding statement that emphasized the tremendous strength of *Near*: "The stays in these cases that have been in effect for more than a week constitute a flouting of the principles of the First Amendment as interpreted in *Near v. Minnesota*."

Justice Black's language, in an opinion joined by Justice Douglas, also echoed some of the discussion during oral arguments in *Near*:

> *Both the history and language of the First Amendment support the view that the press must be left free to publish news, whatever the source, without censorship, injunctions or prior restraints . . . Only a free and unrestrained press can effectively expose deception in government . . . [T]he New York Times, the Washington Post, and other newspapers should be commended for serving the purpose that the Founding Fathers saw so clearly. In revealing the workings of government that led to the Vietnam War, the newspapers did precisely what the founders hoped and trusted they would do.*

Near Is Ever-Present

Even in the dissents in the Pentagon Papers case, *Near* was ubiquitous. Chief Justice Warren Burger, Justice John Harlan and Justice Harry Blackmun in their dissenting opinions also cited Hughes's exceptions to the prohibitions against prior restraint such as interfering with recruiting during wartime and publishing troopship sailing dates. As in *Near*, the Court's judgment in the Pentagon Papers case did not establish the absolutism of the First Amendment (as some journalists still contend) against *all* prior restraints. Justice Byron White wrote: "I do not say that in no circumstances would the First Amendment permit an injunction against publishing information about government plans and operations."

Although it was the judgment of the divided Court that lifted the prior restraint on the *New York Times*, the *Washington Post* and twenty other newspapers, which were prepared to publish sections of the Pentagon Papers, five sentences by District Court Judge Murray Gurfein endure. It is the kind of quotation Colonel McCormick might have had chiseled in his hall:

> The security of the Nation is not at the ramparts alone. Security also lies in the value of our free institutions. A cantankerous press, an obstinate press, a ubiquitous press must be suffered by those in authority in order to preserve the even greater values of freedom of expression and the right of the people to know . . . These are troubled times. There is no greater safety valve for discontent and cynicism about the affairs of Government than freedom of expression in any form.

Gurfein said that he scribbled his opinion "in the light of *Near* with Hughes' opinion in front of me." The Chief Justice had composed his judgment in the light of Madison, who certainly had Blackstone's four-volume commentaries beside him when such concepts as "the freedom of speech and of the press" and "due process" were written into the Bill of Rights.

Good Emerging from Bad

Near v. Minnesota, that yarn stretching from the *Rip-saw* [a Duluth, Minnesota, newspaper that also faced extinction through Minnesota state law] to [Near's] *Saturday Press* to a split court in Washington, reminds us of what great law emerged from those noxious scandal sheets. Or *were* those publications so "malicious, scandalous and defamatory"? Mathias Baldwin, the county judge who imposed the first gag, and Sam Shapiro, the cleaner who considered Near his only champion, might still argue about that judgment. So would Justice Pierce Butler, who was convinced that Near and [his cohort, Howard] Guilford were blackmailers, and McCormick, who thought all Minnesota politicians were crooks.

[Justice Louis] Brandeis would have called the question irrelevant. "These editors ... seek to expose combinations between criminals and public officials ...," he said during the oral arguments. "Now if that campaign was not privileged, if that is not one of the things for which the press exists, then for what does it exist?"

Near was a perilously close case, but "a morsel of genuine history," as [U.S. president/Declaration of Independence author Thomas] Jefferson described such events, "a thing so rare as to be always valuable."

On that afternoon in 1931, few could have predicted the impact that *Near* would have on the half century that followed, particularly the last two decades with the civil rights struggle and the antiwar movement. No other nation on earth has a constitutional tradition against prior restraints comparable to those which sprang from Hughes's sweeping opinion.

But the Constitution is not a self-executing document. The free-press clause and the rest of the Bill of Rights could have remained a benign exhortation. . . .

But history, fate or whatever force it is that provides the unlikely champion, or the subtle, improbable turn of events that leaves its indelible stamp upon the course of human events, intervened. It was one such incident that ultimately empowered five Supreme Court Justices to infuse with life and spirit an amendment which for 150 years had existed only as a bare skeleton.

Victories such as *Near* often pass almost without notice, obscured by the crush of daily events until time affords them their proper stature. Yet the pendulum swings; *Near*'s landmark status will continually be reread in the context of history. Whether its significance is to be upheld or eroded is a question whose answer lies chapters ahead in American law and liberty, in our newsrooms no less than in our courtrooms.

> *"It seems that no prior restraint has come to mean no restraint."*

Near Has Led to Media Excesses

Patrick Buchanan

In Near v. Minnesota, *handed down in 1931, the U.S. Supreme Court deemed unconstitutional a Minnesota state law that allowed judges the right to ban publication of periodicals they considered "lewd" and "scandalous." In the following opinion piece, written at the time of the fiftieth anniversary of the* Near *decision, conservative newspaper columnist and television commentator Patrick Buchanan links* Near *to a more contemporary American culture. While he applauds the decision, Buchanan contends it has led to excessive demands for freedom from censorship. He insists that peddlers of hard-core sex publications should not be guaranteed the same press freedoms as daily newspapers or weekly magazines. Furthermore, he condemns the news media's abuses and excesses. Too often, according to Buchanan, the press successfully evades responsibility for its own scandals. For example, newspapers regularly condemn public officials for their moral transgressions, yet similar misbehavior among journalists goes unreported.*

Live nude dancing, declared Justice Byron White, is a form of free expression, "not without its 1st Amendment protection from official regulation." Six colleagues concurred. Another victory for the 1st Amendment.

At issue was a zoning ordinance in Mt. Ephraim, N.J., said to be violated by the proprietors of a dirty-book store who

Chicago Tribune, June 9, 1981, "Freedom From Any Restraint?" by Patrick Buchanan. Reproduced by permission of the author.

had a coin-operated device on the premises that allowed customers to view nude dancing.

Chief Justice Warren Burger and Justice William Rehnquist dissented:

"The towns and villages of this nation are not and should not be forced into a mold cast by the court . . . Citizens should be free to choose to shape their communities so that it embodies their conception of the 'decent life.'"

". . . To invoke the 1st Amendment to protect the activity involved . . . trivializes and demeans" that amendment.

Any doubt as to which side James Madison would have taken?

Up in the Empire State last month [May 1981], the court decision was anticipated, it would seem, by the Court of Appeals, New York's highest, which struck down a state law written to prevent pornographers from exploiting children. The statute "cannot be sustained," said the court, "since no justification has been shown" other than "special legislative distaste for this type of portrayal."

Timely, that these decisions should come just as the press is celebrating—rightly so—the 50th anniversary of *Near v. Minnesota*, the Supreme Court decision that declared there must be no prior restraint upon the press.

Often, however, it seems that no prior restraint has come to mean no restraint.

Defining the Press

Simple question from one in the minority of the journalistic fraternity: Are pornographers a legitimate part of the press, entitled to the same rights, freedoms, and privileges for what they do, as we are for what we do?

In the increasingly angry conflict between the majority of Americans who want some sort of control—yes, censorship—of this filthy business, are we on the side of the people or on the side of the "1st Amendment rights" of the pornographer? If we are with the latter, we should not be surprised we have won the contempt of the former.

In 1st Amendment Week, perhaps we should examine what the public views as the not occasional sins of the national press.

We demand ironclad protection for the secrecy of our operations, the confidentiality of our sources. Even if you have a search warrant, stay the devil out of our newsrooms. As for the lesser peasantry of business and government, however, what is needed there is constant scrutiny, sunshine laws, document filching, Freedom of Information demands, total access.

We, the press, hold that the private life of public men is fair game. If a congressman is caught with a mistress, or nailed in a sex scandal, we ride him out of town on a rail to spend the rest of his life in penitence and remorse. If, however, one of the princes of our profession is engaged, enthusiastically, in a similar pursuit, we shield him or her as we would a good fraternity brother or sorority sister.

Journalistic Excess?

We will "declassify" at whim the security documents we discover, even if the government servant who did so would face immediate dismissal, and possible indictment. That is our right.

We turn loose the hounds when we sniff out incompetence or misfeasance in a major corporation—especially an oil company. But don't bother sending your reporters around to the Washington Post Co., when the entire episcopate there has been journalistically seduced by a 26-year-old from Toledo named Janet Cooke [a *Post* reporter whose fictitious story about an eight-year-old heroin addict earned a Pulitzer Prize]—because then, brother, you will run into a real stone wall.

We believe in the thorough scrutiny of all powerful institutions, in the interest of the "people's right to know"—except, of course, the most powerful, the press.

We are the watchdogs of the public morality—but no one had better fool around with this watchdog, even when he has conspicuously soiled the rug.

We are the Fourth Estate, the mighty "adversary press," the best paid, most privileged, most pampered, most prestigious journalists in history. We set the national agenda. We produce and direct the public drama in which we cast ourselves as heroic "surrogates of the people," and not infrequently, an "oppressed class"—to a citizenry that must view our antics with an incredulity bordering on utter astonishment.

> "The FCC needs to find better things to do than hunt down profanity."

Even Objectionable Individuals Deserve Press Freedom

Tony Mauro

In 1931, when the Near v. Minnesota *ruling was handed down, the American media primarily consisted of newspapers and magazines. Television, radio, and the Internet have led to new issues related to press freedom and censorship. In the following article, Tony Mauro criticizes efforts to limit sexual content, obscenity, and offensive speech on the airwaves. He observes that contentious media personalities and those who hold controversial political views may offend large segments of the population. By standing up against censorship, however, such individuals— including Jay Near—have helped to secure the First Amendment rights of all Americans.*

Mauro, a journalist, is the Supreme Court correspondent for American Lawyer Media *and* Legal Times.

There's a lot not to love about Howard Stern. Janet Jackson and U2's lead singer, Bono, may not be your favorites, either.

But because the government has decided to target them in a new, censorious war on live broadcasting, all three deserve enthusiastic support. If we let the government win, a dreary world of bleeped, canned and punch-pulling television and radio awaits.

You know the story thus far. It began with Jackson's "wardrobe malfunction" at the [2004] Super Bowl [in which Jackson exposed a breast], which got the attention of Capitol Hill along with thousands of leering boys, young and old. The House of Representatives voted to hike fines for broadcast indecency. The Federal Communications Commission (FCC) leaped into action, too. It slapped $495,000 in fines on Clear Channel for broadcasting a fairly typical, flatulence-filled segment of Stern's radio show. Clear Channel promptly dropped his show from its stations.

Then the FCC found that Bono's spontaneous use of a single expletive during the live broadcast of last year's [2003] Golden Globe Awards was indecent and profane. "This is really, really, f------ brilliant!" is the exclamation by Bono that ultimately upset the FCC.

The Bono edict may be the most troubling of the post–Super Bowl developments. Previously, the FCC's indecency rules—dubious to start with—were enforced only in cases of "deliberate and repetitive" uses of expletives. Now, the commission says that the isolated or fleeting use of taboo words can lead to the revocation of licenses. And it has broadened the definition of forbidden words to include those that are "as highly offensive as the 'F-word.'" Blasphemy, as well as "personally reviling epithets," terms that are vulgar, irreverent and "grossly offensive" will also raise red flags now.

Defining "Offensive"

What do those terms mean?

That's for regulators to imagine and broadcasters to guess at. Legitimate commentary condemning President [George W.] Bush or [2004] Democratic presidential candidate John Kerry, the Palestinians or the Israelis could all be grossly offensive to some, blasphemous to others.

Venezuelan President Hugo Chavez used a word to describe Bush recently that, no matter how it's translated, would fit the definition of fleeting vulgarity. Does that make Chavez's comment less newsworthy?

The coverage of live news and sports events—what baseball or basketball game is profanity-free?—could get a station in trouble. On the famous Super Bowl Sunday night, KCAL in Los Angeles aired a profanity-filled interview with Lakers' star center Shaquille O'Neal. If these rules had been in effect before and during President [Bill] Clinton's impeachment in 1999, the mere reporting of the independent counsel's report, replete with lurid details, might have been deemed off-limits.

Becoming Prudish

Predictably, broadcasters are not taking chances. They are hitting the "dump" or delete button during the airing of talk shows, including [conservative radio talk show host] Rush Limbaugh's, and thinking twice before airing shows as innocuous as *Antiques Roadshow*—which recently featured a lithograph of Marilyn Monroe that might have upset the FCC. LIN Broadcasting is installing tape-delay technology for news broadcasts on its 24 stations. "'When in doubt, leave it out' will inevitably govern in many instances," the Radio-Television News Directors Association warns.

Public broadcasters told the FCC recently that "we have been forced, at increased expense, to provide multiple nationwide feeds of programs that would have been unthinkable to edit only weeks ago." Case in point: deleting strong language in the popular Masterpiece Theatre series from Britain, *Prime Suspect*. "I have given up on PBS," one angry viewer wrote in to protest the self-censorship.

When Americans are becoming more prudish than the Brits, we are truly in trouble.

Censoring Words and Images

As leading First Amendment lawyer Bruce Sanford wrote in a paper for the Media Institute, "The regulations, ungracefully crafted as a sledgehammer instead of with the slick precision of a Ginsu knife, crush expression not just from the lewd and lascivious, but from [British actress] Emma Thompson as well."

The government may not be done with its campaign. It has traditionally left the content of cable television alone because people choose to buy cable. But some in Congress have recently questioned that rationale and are trying to tinker with cable as well. *The Sopranos* without profanity would be like *Fear Factor* without insects. HBO would wither up and die.

All this investigating and knuckle-rapping goes on while the airwaves are awash with other forms of violence and offensiveness. The awful images [of torture] from Abu Ghraib prison in Iraq are punctuated on news shows by wink-wink commercials for Levitra and Cialis [drugs that treat male impotence], complete with references to certain physical phenomena lasting four hours or longer. Spam on the Internet outwits even the worst that Howard Stern can concoct.

The FCC needs to find better things to do than hunt down profanity. And the public needs to show its support for the Sterns and Bonos of the world as they stand against government censorship.

Objectionable People That Stand for Us All

Stern's case may or may not enter the courts, but if it does, he will join a long line of objectionable people who make important First Amendment law that affects the rest of us.

In 1931, the Supreme Court case of a vicious anti-Semitic publisher named Jay Near established the vital rule against prior restraint of the media. In 1988, a vile parody by *Hustler* publisher Larry Flynt became the vehicle for an important Supreme Court ruling protecting satire.

You may find Stern to represent the most objectionable humor and commentary known to man, but in his battle against censorship, he stands for all of us.

CHAPTER 2

Protecting the Press Against Charges of Libel

Chapter Preface

Case Overview: *New York Times v. Sullivan (1964)*

The Supreme Court case of *New York Times v. Sullivan* was decided in the context of the civil rights movement, which began in force during the 1950s and was gathering momentum in 1964, when the Court heard the case. Four years earlier, civil rights advocates had attempted to publicize their struggle for equality by purchasing advertising space in the *New York Times*. Their ad—sponsored by the Committee to Defend Martin Luther King and the Struggle for Freedom in the South—was printed in the paper on March 29, 1960. Its copy began, "As the whole world knows by now, thousands of Southern Negro students are engaged in widespread non-violent demonstrations in positive affirmation of the right to live in human dignity as guaranteed by the U.S. Constitution and the Bill of Rights." It went on to offer examples of police brutality against students in Montgomery, Alabama, and elsewhere. It asserted that "the Southern violators of the Constitution" are "determined to destroy the one man who, more than any other, symbolizes the new spirit sweeping the South—the Rev. Dr. Martin Luther King, Jr."

The advertisement included the names of several dozen supporters, including clergymen, actors (Marlon Brando, Harry Belafonte, Sidney Poitier, Shelley Winters), writers (Lorraine Hansberry, Elmer Rice), and a former First Lady (Eleanor Roosevelt), and solicited donations to aid the cause of civil rights. However, it also contained a number of inaccuracies with relation to police procedure during a protest on the Alabama State College campus and the number of times King had been arrested. L.B. Sullivan, the Montgomery city commissioner who ran the police department, filed a libel suit against the *Times* and four African American clergymen whose names appeared in the ad. Sullivan claimed that the facts stated were erroneous and that his reputation was damaged—even though he was not personally cited in the copy. An Alabama jury heard the case and awarded Sullivan five hundred thousand dollars based on the state's libel law. At the time, the U.S. Supreme Court had not dealt extensively with libel laws, leaving it up to the individual states and their court systems to define libel.

The Alabama State Supreme Court upheld the verdict, but the *Times* and the clergymen appealed to the Supreme Court. The crux of their case involved whether state libel laws violated the freedom of the press guarantee found in the First Amendment. It also took into account the Fourteenth Amendment clause that prohibits states from making or enforcing laws that abridge the privileges and immunities of American citizens.

On March 9, 1964, the Supreme Court announced its decision. The nine-member court unanimously ruled that public officials could only collect damages for libel if they proved in court that accusations made against them were purposefully malicious—that is, made without regard to the truth. The Court justified its new, more difficult standard for proving libel on the grounds that the threat of libel suits only served to inhibit local and national debate over significant issues such as civil rights.

New York Times v. Sullivan is a landmark case. The Court's decision emphasized that reporters and individual citizens may responsibly criticize government officials without fear of being taken to court and accused of slander. Doubts about the ability to prove one's case in a courtroom or fear of financial ruin should not deter a reporter, editor, columnist, or citizen from speaking out against such officials. In 1967 the ruling was broadened to include commentary about other public figures, including actors, athletes, and corporation heads.

> *"The rule of law applied by the Alabama courts is constitutionally deficient for failure to provide . . . safeguards for freedom of . . . the press."*

The Court's Decision: Criticism of Government Is Not Libelous

William J. Brennan Jr.

On March 9, 1964, the U.S. Supreme Court Justices handed down a unanimous ruling in New York Times v. Sullivan. *The case involved a Montgomery, Alabama, police chief who had brought a successful libel suit against the* New York Times *and four African American clergymen based on the content of an advertisement placed in the paper in 1960. In* Sullivan, *the Court overturned that decision and ruled that criticism of a public official can only be deemed libelous if it is knowingly false or made without regard to the truth.*

In this excerpt from the Court's opinion, William J. Brennan Jr. emphatically states that government officials cannot take legal action against newspapers or individuals who criticize their behavior. The threat of such lawsuits inhibits public debate over—and public criticism of—the policies and actions of elected officials, thus denying citizens the right to a free press and free exchange of ideas as guaranteed in the First Amendment. The Court's ruling also prevents states from creating laws that reduce the freedoms and protections of citizens guaranteed in the Fourteenth Amendment.

William J. Brennan Jr., majority opinion, *New York Times v. Sullivan*, 1964.

*New Jersey–born Brennan, an outspoken liberal, was named
to the Supreme Court in 1956. He remained on it until his re-
tirement in 1990 and died seven years later.*

We are required in this case to determine for the first
time the extent to which the constitutional protections
for speech and press limit a State's power to award damages in
a libel action brought by a public official against critics of his
official conduct. . . .

Because of the importance of the constitutional issues involved, we granted the separate petitions for certiorari of the
individual petitioners and of the [*New York*] *Times*. We reverse
the judgment. We hold that the rule of law applied by the Alabama courts is constitutionally deficient for failure to provide
the safeguards for freedom of speech and of the press that are
required by the First and Fourteenth Amendments in a libel
action brought by a public official against critics of his official
conduct. We further hold that, under the proper safeguards,
the evidence presented in this case is constitutionally insufficient to support the judgment for [L.B. Sullivan, the] respondent.

Two Unpersuasive Objections

We may dispose at the outset of two grounds asserted to insulate the judgment of the Alabama courts from constitutional
scrutiny. The first is the proposition relied on by the State Supreme Court—that "The Fourteenth Amendment is directed
against State action, and not private action." That proposition
has no application to this case. Although this is a civil lawsuit
between private parties, the Alabama courts have applied a
state rule of law which petitioners claim to impose invalid restrictions on their constitutional freedoms of speech and press.
It matters not that that law has been applied in a civil action
and that it is common law only, though supplemented by statute. The test is not the form in which state power has been

applied but, whatever the form, whether such power has, in fact, been exercised.

The second contention is that the constitutional guarantees of freedom of speech and of the press are inapplicable here, at least so far as the *Times* is concerned, because the allegedly libelous statements were published as part of a paid, "commercial" advertisement. The argument relies on *Valentine v. Chrestensen* [1942], where the Court held that a city ordinance forbidding street distribution of commercial and business advertising matter did not abridge the First Amendment freedoms, even as applied to a handbill having a commercial message on one side but a protest against certain official action, on the other. The reliance is wholly misplaced. The Court in *Chrestensen* reaffirmed the constitutional protection for "the freedom of communicating information and disseminating opinion"; its holding was based upon the factual conclusions that the handbill was "purely commercial advertising" and that the protest against official action had been added only to evade the ordinance.

The publication here was not a "commercial" advertisement in the sense in which the word was used in *Chrestensen*. It communicated information, expressed opinion, recited grievances, protested claimed abuses, and sought financial support on behalf of a movement whose existence and objectives are matters of the highest public interest and concern. That the *Times* was paid for publishing the advertisement is as immaterial in this connection as is the fact that newspapers and books are sold. Any other conclusion would discourage newspapers from carrying "editorial advertisements" of this type, and so might shut off an important outlet for the promulgation of information and ideas by persons who do not themselves have access to publishing facilities—who wish to exercise their freedom of speech even though they are not members of the press. The effect would be to shackle the First Amendment in its attempt to secure "the widest possible dissemination of information from diverse and antagonistic sources" [as noted in] *Associated Press v. United States* [1945]. To avoid placing such a handicap upon the freedoms of expression, we hold that, if the allegedly libelous statements would otherwise be constitutionally protected from the present judgment, they do not forfeit that protection because they were published in the form of a paid advertisement.

The Alabama Law

Under Alabama law, as applied in this case, a publication is "libelous *per se*" if the words "tend to injure a person . . . in his reputation" or to "bring [him] into public contempt"; the trial court stated that the standard was met if the words are such as to "injure him in his public office, or impute misconduct to him in his office, or want of official integrity, or want of fidelity to a public trust. . . ." The jury must find that the words were published "of and concerning" the plaintiff, but, where the plaintiff is a public official, his place in the governmental hierarchy is sufficient evidence to support a finding that his reputation has been affected by statements that reflect upon the agency of which he is in charge. Once "libel *per se*" has been established, the defendant has no defense as to stated facts unless he can persuade the jury that they were true in all their particulars. His privilege of "fair comment" for expressions of opinion depends on the truth of the facts upon which the comment is based. Unless he can discharge the burden of proving truth, general damages are presumed, and may be awarded without proof of pecuniary injury. A showing of actual malice is apparently a prerequisite to recovery of punitive damages, and the defendant may, in any event, forestall a punitive award by a retraction meeting the statutory requirements. Good motives and belief in truth do not negate an inference of malice, but are relevant only in mitigation of punitive damages if the jury chooses to accord them weight.

A Free Press Issue?

The question before us is whether this rule of liability, as applied to an action brought by a public official against critics of his official conduct, abridges the freedom of speech and of the press that is guaranteed by the First and Fourteenth Amendments.

Respondent relies heavily, as did the Alabama courts, on statements of this Court to the effect that the Constitution does not protect libelous publications. Those statements do not foreclose our inquiry here. None of the cases sustained the use of libel laws to impose sanctions upon expression critical of the official conduct of public officials. The dictum in *Pennekamp v. Florida* [1946], that "when the statements amount to defamation, a judge has such remedy in damages for libel as do other public servants," implied no view as to what remedy might constitutionally be afforded to public officials. In *Beauharnais v. Illinois* [1952], the Court sustained an Illinois criminal libel statute as applied to a publication held to be both defamatory of a racial group and "liable to cause violence and disorder." But the Court was careful to note that it "retains and exercises authority to nullify action which encroaches on freedom of utterance under the guise of punishing libel"; for "public men are, as it were, public property," and "discussion cannot be denied, and the right, as well as the duty, of criticism must not be stifled." *Id.* In the only previous case that did present the question of constitutional limitations upon the power to award damages for libel of a public official, the Court was equally divided and the question was not decided. In deciding the question now, we are compelled by neither precedent nor policy to give any more weight to the epithet "libel" than we have to other "mere labels" of state law. Like insurrection, contempt, advocacy of unlawful acts, breach of the peace, obscenity, solicitation of legal business, and the various other formulae for the repression of expression that have been challenged in this Court, libel can claim no talismanic immunity from constitutional limitations. It must be measured by standards that satisfy the First Amendment.

A Free Flow of Ideas

The general proposition that freedom of expression upon public questions is secured by the First Amendment has long been settled by our decisions. The constitutional safeguard, we have said, "was fashioned to assure unfettered interchange of ideas for the bringing about of political and social changes desired by the people" [as noted in] *Roth v. United States* (1957).

> The maintenance of the opportunity for free political discussion to the end that government may be responsive to the will of the people and that changes may be obtained by lawful means, an opportunity essential to the security of the Republic, is a fundamental principle of our constitutional system. [*Stromberg v. California* (1931).]

"[I]t is a prized American privilege to speak one's mind, although not always with perfect good taste, on all public institutions," [as noted in] *Bridges v. California* [1941], and this opportunity is to be afforded for "vigorous advocacy" no less than "abstract discussion" [as noted in] *NAACP v. Button* [1963]. The First Amendment, said Judge Learned Hand,

> presupposes that right conclusions are more likely to be gathered out of a multitude of tongues than through any kind of authoritative selection. To many, this is, and always will be, folly, but we have staked upon it our all.

The Importance of Public Debate

Mr. Justice [Louis] Brandeis, in his concurring opinion in *Whitney v. California* [1927], gave the principle its classic formulation:

> Those who won our independence believed . . . that public discussion is a political duty, and that this should be a fun-

damental principle of the American government. They recognized the risks to which all human institutions are subject. But they knew that order cannot be secured merely
through fear of punishment for its infraction; that it is haz-
ardous to discourage thought, hope and imagination; that
fear breeds repression; that repression breeds hate; that hate
menaces stable government; that the path of safety lies in
the opportunity to discuss freely supposed grievances and
proposed remedies; and that the fitting remedy for evil coun-
sels is good ones. Believing in the power of reason as applied through public discussion, they eschewed silence co-
erced by law—the argument of force in its worst form.
Recognizing the occasional tyrannies of governing majori-
ties, they amended the Constitution so that free speech and
assembly should be guaranteed.

Thus, we consider this case against the background of a
profound national commitment to the principle that debate
on public issues should be uninhibited, robust, and wide-
open, and that it may well include vehement, caustic, and
sometimes unpleasantly sharp attacks on government and
public officials. The present advertisement, as an expression of
grievance and protest on one of the major public issues of our
time, would seem clearly to qualify for the constitutional protection. The question is whether it forfeits that protection by
the falsity of some of its factual statements and by its alleged
defamation of respondent.

Truth Is Not Required for First Amendment Protection

Authoritative interpretations of the First Amendment guarantees have consistently refused to recognize an exception for
any test of truth—whether administered by judges, juries, or
administrative officials—and especially one that puts the burden of proving truth on the speaker. The constitutional protection does not turn upon "the truth, popularity, or social
utility of the ideas and beliefs which are offered" [as noted in]

NAACP v. Button. As [Founding Father James] Madison said, "Some degree of abuse is inseparable from the proper use of every thing, and in no instance is this more true than in that of the press." In *Cantwell v. Connecticut* [1940], the Court declared:

> In the realm of religious faith, and in that of political belief, sharp differences arise. In both fields, the tenets of one man may seem the rankest error to his neighbor. To persuade others to his own point of view, the pleader, as we know, at times resorts to exaggeration, to vilification of men who have been, or are, prominent in church or state, and even to false statement. But the people of this nation have ordained, in the light of history, that, in spite of the probability of excesses and abuses, these liberties are, in the long view, essential to enlightened opinion and right conduct on the part of the citizens of a democracy.

That erroneous statement is inevitable in free debate, and that it must be protected if the freedoms of expression are to have the "breathing space" that they "need . . . to survive" [as noted in] *NAACP v. Button.* . . .

Only Statements Made with "Actual Malice" Are Libelous

A rule compelling the critic of official conduct to guarantee the truth of all his factual assertions—and to do so on pain of libel judgments virtually unlimited in amount—leads to . . . "self-censorship." Allowance of the defense of truth, with the burden of proving it on the defendant, does not mean that only false speech will be deterred. Even courts accepting this defense as an adequate safeguard have recognized the difficulties of adducing legal proofs that the alleged libel was true in all its factual particulars. Under such a rule, would-be critics of official conduct may be deterred from voicing their criticism, even though it is believed to be true and even though it is in fact true, because of doubt whether it can be proved in court or fear of the expense of having to do so. They tend to make only statements which "steer far wider of the unlawful zone" [as noted in] *Speiser v. Randall* [1958]. The rule thus dampens the vigor and limits the variety of public debate. It is inconsistent with the First and Fourteenth Amendments. The constitutional guarantees require, we think, a federal rule that prohibits a public official from recovering damages for a defamatory falsehood relating to his official conduct unless he proves that the statement was made with "actual malice"— that is, with knowledge that it was false or with reckless disregard of whether it was false or not. . . .

Criticism of Government Does Not Equal Libel

[The Alabama State Supreme Court], in holding that the trial court "did not err in overruling the demurrer [of the *Times*] in the aspect that the libelous matter was not of and concerning the [plaintiff Sullivan,]" based its ruling on the proposition that:

> We think it common knowledge that the average person knows that municipal agents, such as police and firemen, and others, are under the control and direction of the city governing body, and more particularly under the direction and control of a single commissioner. In measuring the performance or deficiencies of such groups, praise or criticism is usually attached to the official in complete control of the body.

This proposition has disquieting implications for criticism of governmental conduct. For good reason,

> no court of last resort in this country has ever held, or even suggested, that prosecutions for libel on government have any place in the American system of jurisprudence. [*City of Chicago v. Tribune Co.* (1923).]

The present proposition would sidestep this obstacle by transmuting criticism of government, however impersonal it may seem on its face, into personal criticism, and hence potential libel, of the officials of whom the government is composed. There is no legal alchemy by which a State may thus create the cause of action that would otherwise be denied for a publication which, as respondent himself said of the advertisement. "reflects not only on me but on the other Commissioners and the community." Raising as it does the possibility that a good-faith critic of government will be penalized for his criticism, the proposition relied on by the Alabama courts strikes at the very center of the constitutionally protected area of free expression. We hold that such a proposition may not constitutionally be utilized to establish that an otherwise impersonal attack on governmental operations was a libel of an official responsible for those operations. Since it was relied on exclusively here, and there was no other evidence to connect the statements with respondent, the evidence was constitutionally insufficient to support a finding that the statements referred to respondent.

"If local power brokers within the South could halt coverage of civil rights by the national media, how could liberal political leaders realistically promise progress toward a more just society?"

Sullivan Was a Victory for Civil Rights

Norman L. Rosenberg

In its 1964 ruling in New York Times v. Sullivan, *the U.S. Supreme Court unanimously decreed that government officials could collect damages in libel suits only if they could prove "actual malice" in the allegations made against them. In this excerpt from his book* Protecting the Best Men: An Interpretive History of the Law of Libel, *Norman L. Rosenberg describes the positive effect of* Sullivan *on the then-burgeoning civil rights movement. Prior to* Sullivan, *southern segregationists had attempted to use libel laws to silence civil rights activists. The Sullivan decision effectively ended such challenges.*

Rosenberg is the DeWitt Wallace Professor of History and Legal Studies at Macalester College in St. Paul, Minnesota.

During the decades that followed World War II, First-Amendment freedoms became a subject of intense legal debate. Free-speech claims, especially those made by people who had run afoul of legislative investigations or who had been charged under the sedition law of 1940 (the Smith Act), initially provoked the most controversy; but eventually the law of political libel also came under scrutiny. . . . By the early 1960s, defamation law became, as it had been in the nineteenth century, a subject for extensive and serious legal debates. The case of *New York Times v. Sullivan* (1964), in which the United States Supreme Court mandated a whole new national approach to defamation law, encapsulated most of the issues surrounding the law of libel; it also reflected many of the social-political-legal dilemmas of mid-twentieth-century liberalism. As always, the law of libel could not be understood apart from the larger history of the time.

"Heed Their Rising Voices"

Times v. Sullivan grew out of the civil rights battles of the 1950s and 1960s, struggles in which activists first converted the streets of the Deep South into free-speech forums and then enlisted the mass media as an ally for attracting new political supporters, especially ones from outside the South. In their challenge to the white southern legal structure, the civil rights movement soon ran headlong into the law of libel.

The most prominent defamation suit resulted from a paid political advertisement entitled "Heed Their Rising Voices," which appeared in the 29 March 1960 issue of the *New York Times*. A plea for funds to finance new campaigns of nonviolent civil disobedience, the advertisement charged officials in Montgomery, Alabama, with repression of civil rights activists and condemned a "reign of terror" by private vigilantes. L. B. Sullivan—a Montgomery police commissioner who claimed that the ad falsely accused him of ordering repressive measures and of inciting violence—sued the *Times* and four prominent black civil rights leaders, including Ralph David Abernathy. "Heed Their Rising Voices" did, in fact, contain substantial inaccuracies, and a trial judge charged an all-white jury that the ad included libelous falsehoods that, under Alabama's conventional defamation laws, were unprotected by any qualified privilege. The jury returned an award of $500,000, and the Alabama Supreme Court sustained the judgment.

A Reflection of the Time

Times v. Sullivan brought together—in legal form—many of the domestic challenges that liberalism faced in the mid-1960s. Certainly the legal issues raised by the libel judgment against the *Times* could not be separated easily from broader questions about the future of civil rights activities. The *Sullivan* suit, as Justice William Brennan noted, was only one of many libel cases involving the civil rights movement. The total value of claims reached more than $6,000,000, and the specter of protracted litigation threatened to pressure even the largest media corporations to self-censor their coverage from the Deep South.

In fact, southern libel laws seemed about to inhibit political discussion even more seriously than had the infamous Sedition Act of 1798. Between 1798 and 1800, it will be recalled, Federalist partisans had failed to stifle political dissent through libel prosecutions; political divisions had run too deep. Thus, when Justice Brennan drew an analogy between the *Sullivan* suit and the Sedition Act prosecutions, he probably understated—rather than exaggerated—the potential for a serious "chill" in the discussion of civil rights issues. The controversy over the mailing of antislavery materials into the South during the 1830s offered a more appropriate historical comparison. Just as nineteenth-century white slaveholders had tried to prevent northern antislavery materials from being mailed into the slave states, so twentieth-century segregationists sought to employ state libel laws to cut off outside criticism of "massive resistance" to racial integration.

Comparison between the 1830s and the 1960s can also help to explain why a sweeping assault on libel law seemed to be the most appropriate response in the *Sullivan* case. During the 1830s, the Democratic party of [President] Andrew Jackson rested upon a proslavery, southern base, and party leaders quickly accepted southern demands that antislavery writers be denied free access to the nation's mails. Conversely, in the 1960s, the civil rights movement found powerful northern support for its claims that traditional libel doctrines unconstitutionally infringed upon freedom of expression.

Eliminating a Tool of Segregation

The *Sullivan* case highlighted the persistence of local resistance not only to the civil rights movement but to the desires of national, agenda-setting elites. As [scholar-authors] Richard Cloward and Frances Fox Piven have suggested, priority-setting elites were determined to channel the civil rights crusade toward issues that could be handled by liberal institutions. The [John F.] Kennedy administration, for example, hoped to convince civil rights leaders that voter registration drives offered greater opportunities, especially for their Democratic party, than broadly focused demonstrations against a variety of different forms of racial discrimination. The political process, prominent liberals repeatedly told young militants, could be made to yield results. But if the technicalities of libel law could be used to mute criticism—or even discussion—of segregationist policies, claims about the openness of the political process were hardly credible. If local power brokers within the South could halt coverage of civil rights by the national media, how could liberal political leaders realistically promise progress toward a more just society? An obvious answer to such questions was to eliminate state libel laws that interfered with discussion of civil rights issues.

Here, the fundamental issue at stake, from the standpoint of black and white activists, was the legitimacy of the larger political process. The brief submitted on behalf of Reverend Abernathy and the other civil rights leaders emphasized this dimension. It characterized the *Sullivan* libel suit as a "further refinement" on "a distinct pattern of resistance" to the "century-long struggle of the Negro people for complete emancipation and full citizenship. . . ." The "flood" of libel suits in Alabama, the Abernathy brief suggested, was "part of a concerted, calculated program to carry out a policy of punishing, intimidating and silencing all who criticize and seek to change Alabama's notorious political system of enforced segregation." Alluding to what civil rights leaders considered the likelihood of similar cases, including slander suits against speakers, the brief claimed that it required "little imagination to picture the destructiveness of such weapons in the hands of those who, only yesterday, used dogs and fire hoses in Birmingham, Alabama, against Negro petitioners leading nonviolent protests against segregation practices." Therefore, the Abernathy brief directly challenged liberals to justify claims that the system really did work and that the guardians of the rule of law could redraw the boundaries of liberty so as to safeguard the rights of blacks and those who preached their cause.

> *"Potentially . . . anyone can be sued any-where for anything posted on the Inter-net."*

Free Press and Libel Law in Cyberspace

Lee Dembart

In 1964 the U.S. Supreme Court unanimously ruled in New York Times v. Sullivan *that government officials must prove "ac-tual malice" in libel suits against newspapers or individuals who criticize their policies or actions. In this opinion piece* Interna-tional Herald Tribune *editor Lee Dembart cites the case while examining the issue of libel suits against journalists who post their reports on the Internet. While the First Amendment to the U.S. Constitution guarantees freedom of the press, legal systems in other countries favor the individual's reputation over the journalist's candor. Dembart fears that the laws of other coun-tries—laws that make it easier to sue for libel—will be applied to the Internet. This development will have a chilling effect on the press, he argues, as publishers will avoid printing material that might result in libel suits. With regard to freedom of the press and the World Wide Web, Dembart prefers the American rule of law as outlined in* Sullivan.

Every person who uses the Internet should be concerned about legal developments . . . that will affect what every-one everywhere can say and read online.

Technology almost always outpaces the ability of law to deal with the changes it brings, and it takes a while for the

Lee Dembart, "Freeing Speech: Whose Rules Will Govern This Worldwide Internet," International Herald Tribune, December 30, 2002, p. 11. Copyright © 2002 by The New York Times Company. Reprinted with permission.

laws to catch up with new ways of doing things. This has proved especially true [since the early 1990s], as cyberspace has become an essential part of world commerce and discourse.

For several years now, courts in various countries have sought to impose their own national laws on the Internet, which by its very nature knows no national boundaries. But that process took a giant leap [in December 2002] . . . when Australia's High Court became the highest court anywhere to endorse the view that the World Wide Web should be governed by the laws of one country—in this case, Australia.

The issue involved a defamation suit brought by an Australian businessman against Dow Jones & Co. for an article published in *Barron's*, posted on its Web site and readable anywhere in the world. Because the U.S. Constitution contains the First Amendment ("Congress shall make no law . . . abridging the freedom of speech or of the press"), U.S. defamation law is very defendant-friendly. So Dow Jones had argued that publication had occurred in New Jersey, the home of the computers that physically contained the article in its electronic form, and that a defamation suit should be brought there. Neither Australia nor Britain has a First Amendment or anything equivalent to it, and their defamation laws are very plaintiff-friendly. So the Australian businessman had argued that since it was possible to download and read the offending article in Australia, his reputation was defamed where he lived and worked, namely in Australia. Australia's High Court sided with him, and the case will proceed in Australia.

The "Chilling Effect"

The decision has correctly sent a chill down the spine of people around the world because it potentially means that anyone can be sued anywhere for anything posted on the Internet. It could mean that the most restrictive laws anywhere in the world will become the law of the Internet. The "chilling effect" of such a regime is clear: No one will be willing to say anything worth reading for fear of running afoul of somebody's laws.

To be sure, while there are millions of Web sites available online, the majority of people who use the Internet don't post anything of their own, so their freedom of speech would not be directly affected. But their freedom to read things would be severely restricted because anything that might lead to a lawsuit would not be posted in the first place.

In fact, the situation would not be quite so severe, particularly for individuals, since, as a practical matter, people would only be sued in jurisdictions where they maintained assets that could be seized to pay a judgment if they lost. I am personally not too worried about being sued in Australia because as far as I know I have nothing there, so a judgment against me couldn't be enforced. Dow Jones, however, and other large media companies may be more vulnerable. And as a passive user of the Internet, I worry that this extraordinary global medium will be hamstrung if everyone now has to think twice or three times before posting anything for fear of being sued somewhere.

The previous cases of countries trying to impose their laws on the Internet—starting with France barring Yahoo from allowing Nazi memorabilia to be auctioned on its Web site—presented the question, but the Australia defamation case puts it most starkly. What we have is a fundamental clash between legal systems and worldviews. What's more, these are not phony-baloney legal systems set up by dictatorships to give the imprimatur of law to repressive governments. These are well-developed, functioning legal systems in countries whose citizens view them as basically fair.

Contrasting Points of View on Libel

In the Australian-British legal mind, individuals have a right to protect their reputations, and people know that if they say or write something that harms someone's reputation, they can be held to account for it and forced to pay damages. In deciding defamation cases, the legal system puts its thumb on the scale of individual reputations.

In the American legal mind, by contrast, society's interest in free and open debate on matters of public interest is held to be more important than individual reputations, particularly in the case of public officials or public figures. Justice William Brennan of the U.S. Supreme Court gave voice to the American view in 1964 in the case of *New York Times v. Sullivan*, in which he wrote of "the profound national commitment to the principle that debate on public issues should be uninhibited, robust and wide open, and that it may well include vehement, caustic and sometimes unpleasantly sharp attacks on government and public officials." In general, the American legal system puts its thumb on the scale of open public debate rather than individual reputations.

Personally, I like that view better. I can hear all of you saying: "Of course you favor the press. You're the press." That's true. But I favor everyone's right to speak freely, and now that we have the Internet, which is used by hundreds of millions of people every day, this is not merely theoretical. I favor free speech for everyone over almost all objections, and the Internet makes that a reality. I don't want to point the finger at Australia's High Court alone and say that it is usurping its jurisdiction by attempting to force the Internet to comply with its laws. American courts do exactly the same thing in matters of copyright, for example, where they consistently apply American law to the international medium. It is crystal clear that what is needed are new global treaties for the Internet so that clashing legal systems can be reconciled. And it is equally clear that the public debate leading up to those treaties should be as uninhibited, robust and wide open as possible.

> "New York Times v. Sullivan was about the suppression of speech in the South [during the 1960s]. Today's version of suppression is just another verse of the same song."

The Lesson of *Sullivan* Has Been Forgotten

Gilbert S. Merritt

In October 2004 Gilbert S. Merritt, a senior circuit judge on the U.S. Court of Appeals for the Sixth Circuit Court in Nashville, Tennessee, was the keynote speaker at New York Times v. Sullivan: Forty Years After, *a conference sponsored by the School of Law and the School of Journalism and Communication at the University of Oregon. In the speech, excerpted here, Merritt argues that the lesson of* Sullivan—*that a free press is essential in a democracy—has been eroded in the ensuing decades. The post–September 11, 2001, war on terror has led the U.S. government to attempt to control the flow of information to its citizens. This effort has resulted in the manipulation and intimidation of journalists and the undermining of civil liberties, and the press has failed to protest these developments. Merritt concludes that journalists need to relearn the purpose of the First Amendment as embodied in* Sullivan.

In an unusual and unexplained set of biological mutations, our evolutionary ancestors in Africa invented speech over 200,000 years ago. Then in the Cradle of Civilization, the Tigris and Euphrates Valley in present day Iraq, the legendary

Gilbert S. Merritt, *Speech at the University of Oregon*, Nashville, TN: 2004. Reproduced by permission of the author.

Garden of Eden in the literature of Muslims, Christians and Jews, our cousins invented written speech 5,000 years ago.

I am sure that as soon as speech was invented, efforts to suppress and control it began, and that process of suppression continues unabated. Hammurabi and Nebuchadnezzar did not tolerate seditious speech any more than Saddam Hussein. Now even our own government regards as seditious speech the leaking of classified information that should have been public all along. And journalists are going to jail.

The serious danger to First Amendment values no longer comes from libel laws but from a different direction. Let me explain.

At the invitation of our government, I spent the summer of 2003 in Iraq as a judicial adviser interviewing a host of then unemployed Iraqi judges and lawyers. There were about 25 Americans, mostly prosecutors, public defenders and court officials, in our law trained group.

Suppressing Speech in Iraq

The American occupation authority had its own website, and two of the lawyers in our group decided to put up a website of personal photographs of our group with captions, describing sights and scenes and events from our summer vacation in Iraq. A few of the pictures were irreverent, funny, risqué, critical.

Mid-level officials in the Defense Department and the Justice Department ordered my friends to remove the website "as a matter of national security." At the request of the group, I wrote a letter to the officials in Washington who gave the order. The letter pointed out that we were not in the military, there was no conceivable national security problem and that the group remained American citizens with rights of free speech, including the right to put on line this kind of photograph website for family and friends back home. I asked the officials to give us some legal basis for this deprivation of First

Amendment rights. No response. My colleagues, some of whom work for the government, feared reprisals and removed the website.

During the months I was there I wrote a number of articles for my local daily newspaper, the *Nashville Tennessean*. A few of the articles were critical, describing what seemed obvious to anyone on the scene, the lack of any plan to stop the looting of Baghdad, no plan to create a constitution-making process or to create electoral machinery so that we could soon turn the government back over to the Iraqis.

Then a week before I left Baghdad . . . on my way home, the Coalition Provisional Authority, under the jurisdiction of the Defense Department, issued an order forbidding people associated with the occupation from providing any information to the press without prior clearance from a special office of the occupation authority. It was important, we were told, that the Americans "stay on message." And the scope of the order included advisers like me. That week I wrote a story for my local newspaper with the lead "This is my last story from Baghdad," pointing out the irony of the order suppressing speech in light of our announced purpose of creating a constitutional democracy in Iraq including free speech and a free press. I did not seek approval or advanced clearance for this story.

Undermining Freedom in the Name of Security

My two personal vignettes about free speech in Iraq are minor symptoms of what is to me the broader tendency spreading across the land. The founding generation warned us many times at the end of the 18th Century to beware of war, large standing armies and the predisposition of the military mind to always choose order over freedom. In *The Federalist Papers*, [American statesman Alexander] Hamilton said, "The continual effort and alarm attendant on the state of war or continual danger will compel nations the most attached to liberty, to resort for repose and security to institutions which have a tendency to destroy their civil and political rights."

As a result of the new, permanent war on terror, we are beginning to see the *New York Times* and a number of reporters having to defend themselves from the government's attempt to subpoena reporters' telephone records because they are gathering news from Islamic charities and other Muslims. The war is producing an assault on the reporter's privilege to maintain the confidentiality of sources. The obsession with national security today is inevitably leading to the same kind of political climate that produced the Pentagon Papers case and the alien and sedition laws.

We also see this tendency to undermine free speech and association in the name of national security in the policy of the Justice Department and the Defense Department to lock up Muslims in Cuba indefinitely without allowing them to speak to family members or lawyers or to test the legality of their incarceration in court. The same policy was applied to American citizens like [Yaser Esam] Hamdi, held incognito and deprived of the right to speak to family or lawyers or anyone else except interrogators.

There was no Hamilton or [Thomas] Jefferson to protest. There was little outcry from any elected official objecting to incognito, incommunicado incarceration.

A conservative Supreme Court finally had to tell Washington ... that this policy of imprisonment and punishment without trial, holding people incommunicado without the right of free speech or counsel, violated our most basic political and personal rights. In Hamdi's case, the most conservative justice and the most liberal, [Antonin] Scalia and [John Paul] Stevens, joined to condemn such indefinite incarceration. ...

The Alien and Sedition Acts and free speech and civil liberties were a major issue in the [presidential] campaign of

1800 that elected Thomas Jefferson over John Adams. But two centuries later no one [seemed] ... sufficiently interested in such issues to even bring up free speech and civil liberties issues for discussion in the [2004 presidential] ... election. The Supreme Court decisions were merely a one-day news story.

The Supression of Information

Nor is either party interested in talking about the massive suppression of publicly-owned information through our security classification system that keeps secret millions of reports and documents containing information valuable to the press and the public.

Even the report of the National Intelligence Council of [2002] ... predicting accurately the insurgency we would face in Iraq is still a secret. And I cannot get released from classification a report on the pre-war judicial system in Iraq compiled in the State Department before the war. All this information ought to be open to the public, but it can only be revealed to the public through leaks. The government then regards the publication of this publicly-owned information in the press as seditious speech. Journalists are then harassed and threatened with jail because they decline to reveal their confidential sources.

Nor has there been any serious discussion of the segregation of protestors against the candidates of either party, the segregation of political dissenters into small compounds out of earshot or eyesight of the events they are protesting. Nor has there been any serious discussion of the arrest of dissenters at a convention, protestors who simply hold up an opposition sign. In the 1960s, the civil rights marchers were marching through the streets of Nashville, Montgomery [Alabama] and many other Southern cities to protest, but now protestors are placed behind fences in out of the way places.

Neither party seems to really object to confining protestors or to the policy of incommunicado incarceration that the Supreme Court held unconstitutional or to object to the security classification system that allows everything to be classified without any remedy, except leaks to journalists.

To Defend Our Democratic Faith

New York Times v. Sullivan was about the suppression of speech in the South [during the 1960s].

Today's version of suppression is just another verse of the same song.

Why should we as lawyers and journalists and judges worry about these kinds of abridgements of free speech?

[Judge] Learned Hand in a case 60 years ago gave us the answer:

> The First Amendment presupposes that right conclusions are more likely to be gathered out of a multitude of tongues than through any kind of authoritative selection. To many this is and always will be folly, but we have staked upon it our all.

That is our Democratic faith, and it is up to lawyers, journalists and judges to enforce it. Our Founding Fathers were the first to articulate the reasons for their First Amendment, the same reasons given by Learned Hand, and by Justice [William J.] Brennan [Jr.] in *New York Times v. Sullivan*. It is a lesson we keep forgetting and must relearn in each succeeding generation.

CHAPTER 3

Balancing Press Freedom and National Security

Chapter Preface

Case Overview: *New York Times Company v. United States* (the Pentagon Papers case) (1971) The U.S. Supreme Court case of *New York Times Company v. United States* grew out of the presidency of Richard Nixon (who became America's thirty-seventh chief executive in 1968), United States involvement in the Vietnam War, and the antiwar movement that was expanding across the country in the late 1960s and early 1970s. Its roots can be traced to Daniel Ellsberg, a U.S. Defense Department employee who had come to view the war as wrongheaded. Ellsberg had access to classified documents totaling seven thousand pages and containing top-secret information regarding America's Vietnam policy as it had evolved between 1945 and 1968. The bulk of the material was titled "History of U.S. Decision-Making Process on Vietnam Policy." It included examples of secrecy and miscommunication between the branches of the federal government and lies told to the American public by government officials, including Harry S. Truman, Dwight D. Eisenhower, John F. Kennedy, and Lyndon B. Johnson, the U.S. presidents who preceded Nixon in office.

Ellsberg photocopied these documents and leaked them to the *New York Times* and *Washington Post*. They came to be known as the Pentagon Papers. On June 13, 1971, excerpts began appearing in the *Times*. Additional material was printed on June 14 and 15.

The Nixon administration, embarrassed by the revelations, denounced the publication as a breach of national security. Administration officials claimed that if the courts did not order the immediate and permanent cessation of the documents' publication, irreparable harm would result. They argued that the war might be lengthened and the safety of America's front-line soldiers would be endangered.

The U.S. Justice Department endeavored to obtain a court order preventing the *Times* from printing additional installments. This marked the first time that the federal government had attempted to censor a newspaper on the grounds of national security. The *Times* argued that publication of the papers was shielded by the First Amendment, which affords the press the protection it requires to uncover any facts surrounding government impropriety, serve and inform the citizenry, and flourish in a democratic society.

Judge Murray I. Gurfein of the U.S. District Court for the Southern District of New York ruled that public dissemination of the papers would not threaten the nation's security. But he issued a temporary restraining order directing the *Times* to halt publication while the Justice Department filed an appeal with the U.S. Court of Appeals for the Second Circuit. This court reversed Gurfein's ruling and ordered the *Times* to cease publishing the papers.

Meanwhile, on June 18 and 19, the *Washington Post* printed sections of the papers, and the Justice Department sought a similar court order halting their publication in that newspaper. However, the U.S. Court of Appeals for the District of Columbia decided not to stop publication. Given the immediacy of the issue, the U.S. Supreme Court consented to consider both cases, which were combined under *New York Times Company v. United States*. Hearings began on June 26.

On June 30 the Court, in a six-to-three decision, allowed the publication of the Pentagon Papers to continue. The Court ruled that the government had not shown adequate cause to justify prior restraint of the documents on national security grounds. While publication might cause discomfort to those cited in the papers, it would not endanger American lives or damage national security.

The *Times, Post,* and other periodicals now were free to publish the material. Before the end of 1971 the Pentagon Papers were also released in book form. Their unimpeded publication added to the already decreasing public backing of the Vietnam War. Primarily, however, the Supreme Court ruling in *New York Times Company v. United States* reaffirmed the right to a free press as guaranteed in the First Amendment.

The Court's Decision: The Press Must Be Free to Criticize the Government

Hugo L. Black

In New York Times Company v. United States *(1971), the U.S. Supreme Court decreed that the* New York Times *and* Washington Post *be allowed to continue publication of the Pentagon Papers, a secret government history of the Vietnam War. The following selection is excerpted from the majority opinion, authored by Hugo L. Black. He proclaims that the suppression of the papers is a direct violation of the First Amendment right to freedom of the press. According to Black, the administration of President Richard M. Nixon used the false premise that the documents' publication would threaten national security as an excuse to prevent criticism of the government's Vietnam policy. However, the First Amendment was created precisely to ensure that such criticisms could take place.*

Black, an Alabama native and former U.S. senator, was a Supreme Court justice for thirty-four years. He enjoyed a reputation as a fervent defender of the freedoms afforded by the U.S. Constitution. He died on September 25, 1971, three months after the following opinion was announced.

I adhere to the view that the Government's case against the *Washington Post* should have been dismissed, and that the injunction against the *New York Times* should have been va-

Hugo L. Black, majority opinion, *New York Times Company v. United States*, 1971.

cated without oral argument when the cases were first presented to this Court. I believe that every moment's continuance of the injunctions against these newspapers amounts to a flagrant, indefensible, and continuing violation of the First Amendment. Furthermore, after oral argument, I agree completely that we must affirm the judgment of the Court of Appeals for the District of Columbia Circuit and reverse the judgment of the Court of Appeals for the Second Circuit for the reasons stated by my Brothers [William] Douglas and [William] Brennan. In my view, it is unfortunate that some of my Brethren are apparently willing to hold that the publication of news may sometimes be enjoined. Such a holding would make a shambles of the First Amendment.

Our Government was launched in 1789 with the adoption of the Constitution. The Bill of Rights, including the First Amendment, followed in 1791. Now, for the first time in the 182 years since the founding of the Republic, the federal courts are asked to hold that the First Amendment does not mean what it says, but rather means that the Government can halt the publication of current news of vital importance to the people of this country.

The Purpose of the Bill of Rights

In seeking injunctions against these newspapers, and in its presentation to the Court, the Executive Branch seems to have forgotten the essential purpose and history of the First Amendment. When the Constitution was adopted, many people strongly opposed it because the document contained no Bill of Rights to safeguard certain basic freedoms. They especially feared that the new powers granted to a central government might be interpreted to permit the government to curtail freedom of religion, press, assembly, and speech. In response to an overwhelming public clamor, James Madison offered a series of amendments to satisfy citizens that these great liberties would remain safe and beyond the power of government to abridge. Madison proposed what later became the First Amendment in three parts, two of which are set out below, and one of which proclaimed:

> The people shall not be deprived or abridged of their right to speak, to write, or to publish their sentiments, *and the freedom of the press, as one of the great bulwarks of liberty, shall be inviolable.* (Emphasis added.)

The amendments were offered to curtail and restrict the general powers granted to the Executive, Legislative, and Judicial Branches two years before in the original Constitution. The Bill of Rights changed the original Constitution into a new charter under which no branch of government could abridge the people's freedoms of press, speech, religion, and assembly. Yet the Solicitor General [Erwin Griswold, who presented the case for the government] argues and some members of the Court appear to agree that the general powers of the Government adopted in the original Constitution should be interpreted to limit and restrict the specific and emphatic guarantees of the Bill of Rights adopted later. I can imagine no greater perversion of history. Madison and the other Framers of the First Amendment, able men that they were, wrote in language they earnestly believed could never be misunderstood: "Congress shall make no law . . . abridging the freedom . . . of the press. . . ." Both the history and language of the First Amendment support the view that the press must be left free to publish news, whatever the source, without censorship, injunctions, or prior restraints.

The Importance of a Free Press

In the First Amendment, the Founding Fathers gave the free press the protection it must have to fulfill its essential role in our democracy. The press was to serve the governed, not the governors. The Government's power to censor the press was abolished so that the press would remain forever free to censure the Government. The press was protected so that it could bare the secrets of government and inform the people. Only a free and unrestrained press can effectively expose deception in government. And paramount among the responsibilities of a free press is the duty to prevent any part of the government from deceiving the people and sending them off to distant lands to die of foreign fever and foreign shot and shell. In my view, far from deserving condemnation for their courageous reporting, the *New York Times*, the *Washington Post*, and other newspapers should be commended for serving the purpose that the Founding Fathers saw so clearly. In revealing the workings of government that led to the Vietnam war, the newspapers nobly did precisely that which the Founders hoped and trusted they would do.

The Government's Case

The Government's case here is based on premises entirely different from those that guided the Framers of the First Amendment. The Solicitor General has carefully and emphatically stated:

> Now, Mr. Justice [Black], your construction of . . . [the First Amendment] is well known, and I certainly respect it. You say that no law means no law, and that should be obvious. I can only say, Mr. Justice, that to me it is equally obvious that "no law" does not mean "no law," and I would seek to persuade the Court that that is true. . . . [T]here are other parts of the Constitution that grant powers and responsibilities to the Executive, and . . . the First Amendment was not intended to make it impossible for the Executive to function or to protect the security of the United States.

And the Government argues in its brief that, in spite of the First Amendment,

> [t]he authority of the Executive Department to protect the nation against publication of information whose disclosure

would endanger the national security stems from two inter-related sources: the constitutional power of the President over the conduct of foreign affairs and his authority as Commander-in-Chief.

A Threat to the First Amendment

In other words, we are asked to hold that, despite the First Amendment's emphatic command, the Executive Branch, the Congress, and the Judiciary can make laws enjoining publication of current news and abridging freedom of the press in the name of "national security." The Government does not even attempt to rely on any act of Congress. Instead, it makes the bold and dangerously far-reaching contention that the courts should take it upon themselves to "make" a law abridging freedom of the press in the name of equity, presidential power and national security, even when the representatives of the people in Congress have adhered to the command of the First Amendment and refused to make such a law. To find that the President has "inherent power" to halt the publication of news by resort to the courts would wipe out the First Amendment and destroy the fundamental liberty and security of the very people the Government hopes to make "secure." No one can read the history of the adoption of the First Amendment without being convinced beyond any doubt that it was injunctions like those sought here that Madison and his collaborators intended to outlaw in this Nation for all time.

The word "security" is a broad, vague generality whose contours should not be invoked to abrogate the fundamental law embodied in the First Amendment. The guarding of military and diplomatic secrets at the expense of informed representative government provides no real security for our Republic. The Framers of the First Amendment, fully aware of both the need to defend a new nation and the abuses of the English and Colonial governments, sought to give this new society strength and security by providing that freedom of speech, press, religion, and assembly should not be abridged. This thought was eloquently expressed in 1937 by Mr. Chief Justice [Charles Evans] Hughes—great man and great Chief Justice that he was—when the Court held a man could not be punished for attending a meeting run by Communists.

> The greater the importance of safeguarding the community from incitements to the overthrow of our institutions by force and violence, the more imperative is the need to preserve inviolate the constitutional rights of free speech, free press and free assembly in order to maintain the opportunity for free political discussion, to the end that government may be responsive to the will of the people and that changes, if desired, may be obtained by peaceful means. Therein lies the security of the Republic, the very foundation of constitutional government.

> "The scope of the judicial function in passing upon the activities of the Executive Branch . . . in the field of foreign affairs is very narrowly restricted."

Dissenting Opinion: The Government Can Suppress Sensitive Information

John Marshall Harlan II

In 1971 three U.S. Supreme Court justices—Chief Justice Warren E. Burger along with Harry A. Blackmun and John Marshall Harlan II—dissented from the majority opinion in New York Times Company v. United States. *The majority view was that the administration of President Richard M. Nixon, in its effort to suppress publication of the Pentagon Papers, was attempting to subvert the First Amendment. In his minority opinion, excerpted here, Harlan criticizes the lack of time afforded the Court to ponder this particular case. The Pentagon Papers consist of thousands of pages of classified material, he contends, which need to be carefully examined to determine if their publication truly endangers the nation's security. In any case, according to Harlan, the judicial branch must defer to the executive in the area of foreign policy because national defense and international affairs are the executive branch's responsibility.*

The Chicago-born Harlan—whose grandfather, John Marshall Harlan, also served on the Supreme Court—joined the Court in 1955. New York Times Company v. United States *was one of his final cases. He left the Court in September 1971 and died on December 29, 1971.*

John Marshall Harlan II, dissenting opinion, *New York Times Company v. United States*, 1971.

These cases forcefully call to mind the wise admonition of Mr. Justice [Oliver Wendell] Holmes, dissenting in *Northern Securities Co. v. United States* (1904):

> Great cases, like hard cases, make bad law. For great cases are called great not by reason of their real importance in shaping the law of the future, but because of some accident of immediate overwhelming interest which appeals to the feelings and distorts the judgment. These immediate interests exercise a kind of hydraulic pressure which makes what previously was clear seem doubtful, and before which even well settled principles of law will bend.

A Feverish Pace

With all respect, I consider that the Court has been almost irresponsibly feverish in dealing with these cases.

Both the Court of Appeals for the Second Circuit and the Court of Appeals for the District of Columbia Circuit rendered judgment on June 23 [1971]. *The New York Times'* petition for certiorari, its motion for accelerated consideration thereof, and its application for interim relief were filed in this Court on June 24 at about 11 a.m. The application of the United States for interim relief in the [*Washington*] *Post* case was also filed here on June 24 at about 7:15 p.m. This Court's order setting a hearing before us on June 26 at 11 a.m., a course which I joined only to avoid the possibility of even more peremptory action by the Court, was issued less than 24 hours before. The record in the *Post* case was filed with the Clerk shortly before 1 p.m. on June 25; the record in the *Times* case did not arrive until 7 or 8 o'clock that same night. The briefs of the parties were received less than two hours before argument on June 26.

This frenzied train of events took place in the name of the presumption against prior restraints created by the First Amendment. Due regard for the extraordinarily important and difficult questions involved in these litigations should have led the Court to shun such a precipitate timetable. In order to decide the merits of these cases properly, some or all of the following questions should have been faced:

Unanswered Questions

1. Whether the Attorney General is authorized to bring these suits in the name of the United States. . . .

2. Whether the First Amendment permits the federal courts to enjoin publication of stories which would present a serious threat to national security.

3. Whether the threat to publish highly secret documents is of itself a sufficient implication of national security to justify an injunction on the theory that, regardless of the contents of the documents, harm enough results simply from the demonstration of such a breach of secrecy.

4. Whether the unauthorized disclosure of any of these particular documents would seriously impair the national security.

5. What weight should be given to the opinion of high officers in the Executive Branch of the Government with respect to questions 3 and 4.

6. Whether the newspapers are entitled to retain and use the documents notwithstanding the seemingly uncontested facts that the documents, or the originals of which they are duplicates, were purloined from the Government's possession, and that the newspapers received them with knowledge that they had been feloniously acquired.

7. Whether the threatened harm to the national security or the Government's possessory interest in the documents justifies the issuance of an injunction against publication in light of—

a. The strong First Amendment policy against prior restraints on publication;

b. The doctrine against enjoining conduct in violation of criminal statutes; and

c. The extent to which the materials at issue have apparently already been otherwise disseminated.

Rush to Judgment

These are difficult questions of fact, of law, and of judgment; the potential consequences of erroneous decision are enormous. The time which has been available to us, to the lower courts, and to the parties has been wholly inadequate for giving these cases the kind of consideration they deserve. It is a reflection on the stability of the judicial process that these great issues—as important as any that have arisen during my time on the Court—should have been decided under the pressures engendered by the torrent of publicity that has attended these litigations from their inception.

Forced as I am to reach the merits of these cases, I dissent from the opinion and judgments of the Court. Within the severe limitations imposed by the time constraints under which I have been required to operate, I can only state my reasons in telescoped form, even though, in different circumstances, I would have felt constrained to deal with the cases in the fuller sweep indicated above.

It is a sufficient basis for affirming the Court of Appeals for the Second Circuit in the *Times* litigation to observe that its order [preventing publication of the documents] must rest on the conclusion that, because of the time elements the Government had not been given an adequate opportunity to present its case to the District Court. At the least this conclusion was not an abuse of discretion.

In the *Post* litigation, the Government had more time to prepare; this was apparently the basis for the refusal of the Court of Appeals for the District of Columbia Circuit on rehearing to conform its judgment to that of the Second Circuit. But I think there is another and more fundamental reason why this judgment cannot stand—a reason which also furnishes an additional ground for not reinstating the judgment of the District Court in the *Times* litigation, set aside by the Court of Appeals. It is plain to me that the scope of the judicial function in passing upon the activities of the Executive Branch of the Government in the field of foreign affairs is very narrowly restricted. This view is, I think, dictated by the concept of separation of powers upon which our constitutional system rests.

Executive Power and Foreign Policy

In a speech on the floor of the House of Representatives [in 1800], Chief Justice John Marshall, then a member of that body, stated:

> The President is the sole organ of the nation in its external relations, and its sole representative with foreign nations.

From that time, shortly after the founding of the Nation, to this, there has been no substantial challenge to this description of the scope of executive power.

From this constitutional primacy in the field of foreign affairs, it seems to me that certain conclusions necessarily follow. Some of these were stated concisely by President [George] Washington, declining the request of the House of Representatives for the papers leading up to the negotiation of the Jay Treaty:

> The nature of foreign negotiations requires caution, and their success must often depend on secrecy; and even when brought to a conclusion, a full disclosure of all the measures, demands, or eventual concessions which may have been proposed or contemplated would be extremely impolitic; for this might have a pernicious influence on future negotiations, or produce immediate inconveniences, perhaps danger and mischief, in relation to other powers.

Proper Role of Judiciary in Foreign Affairs

The power to evaluate the "pernicious influence" of premature disclosure is not, however, lodged in the Executive alone. I agree that, in performance of its duty to protect the values of the First Amendment against political pressures, the judiciary must review the initial Executive determination to the point of satisfying itself that the subject matter of the dispute does lie within the proper compass of the President's foreign relations power. Constitutional considerations forbid "a complete abandonment of judicial control." [*United States v. Reynolds* (1953).] Moreover, the judiciary may properly insist that the determination that disclosure of the subject matter would irreparably impair the national security be made by the head of the Executive Department concerned—here, the Secretary of State or the Secretary of Defense—after actual personal consideration by that officer. This safeguard is required in the analogous area of executive claims of privilege for secrets of state.

But, in my judgment, the judiciary may not properly go beyond these two inquiries and redetermine for itself the probable impact of disclosure on the national security.

> [T]he very nature of executive decisions as to foreign policy is political, not judicial. Such decisions are wholly confided by our Constitution to the political departments of the government, Executive and Legislative. They are delicate, complex, and involve large elements of prophecy. They are and should be undertaken only by those directly responsible to the people whose welfare they advance or imperil. They are decisions of a kind for which the Judiciary has neither aptitude, facilities nor responsibility, and which has long been held to belong in the domain of political power not subject to judicial intrusion or inquiry. [*Chicago & Southern Air Lines v. Waterman Steamship Corp.* (1948).]

A Need for Further Review

Even if there is some room for the judiciary to override the executive determination, it is plain that the scope of review must be exceedingly narrow. I can see no indication in the opinions of either the District Court or the Court of Appeals in the *Post* litigation that the conclusions of the Executive were given even the deference owing to an administrative agency, much less than owing to a co-equal branch of the Government operating within the field of its constitutional prerogative.

Accordingly, I would vacate the judgment of the Court of Appeals for the District of Columbia Circuit [allowing publication of the Pentagon Papers in the *Washington Post*] on this ground, and remand the case for further proceedings in the District Court. Before the commencement of such further proceedings, due opportunity should be afforded the Government for procuring from the Secretary of State or the Secretary of Defense or both an expression of their views on the issue of national security. The ensuing review by the District Court should be in accordance with the views expressed in this opinion. And, for the reasons stated above, I would affirm the judgment of the Court of Appeals for the Second Circuit [preventing publication of the Pentagon Papers in the *New York Times*].

Pending further hearings in each case conducted under the appropriate ground rules, I would continue the restraints on publication. I cannot believe that the doctrine prohibiting prior restraints reaches to the point of preventing courts from maintaining the *status quo* long enough to act responsibly in matters of such national importance as those involved here.

Press and Public Reaction to *New York Times v. United States*

Alexander Auerbach

*On June 30, 1971, the U.S. Supreme Court rendered its opinion
in* New York Times Company v. United States, *with the majority ruling that the administration of President Richard M. Nixon
had not displayed sufficient grounds for preventing publication
of the Pentagon Papers. On July 4 the* Los Angeles Times *published a news item that measured the reaction to the decision. Its
author,* Times *staff writer Alexander Auerbach, cites an array of
newspaper editorials, columnists, prominent individuals, letters
to editors, and public opinion polls.*

*Even though the Court decision was pro–freedom of the
press, the article points out that not all newspapers hailed the result. Some questioned the illegal manner in which the Pentagon
Papers were obtained. Others stressed that the papers were labeled "top secret" and claimed that their publication was a
threat to national security. Conversely, quite a few of those sur-
veyed backed the* New York Times *and* Washington Post's *decision to publish the papers. They expressed the viewpoint that the
government keeps too much information secret and that the*

Alexander Auerbach, "Pentagon Papers: The Press Stands—Slightly Divided," Los Angeles Times, July 4, 1971, p. C9. Copyright © Los Angeles Times. All rights reserved.
Reprinted with permission.

public's right to know is paramount in a free society. In conclusion, both the press and the public had a mixed reaction to the ruling.

Crisis, like politics, produces strange bedfellows; and the conflict over the publication of the so-called Pentagon Papers produced some of the strangest.

Lester Maddox and George Wallace spoke out for the *New York Times* despite their hostility toward its liberal views. A conservative Republican paper called the Nixon Administration "inept and stupid." The *Wall Street Journal* editorialized in defense of taking of government information, although not government property.

Pierre Salinger, who when he was a Presidential press secretary [in the administration of John F. Kennedy] was obliged to joust with the press, defended press efforts to dig out secret information in his new role of columnist.

And some columnists peeked under the press' mantle of righteousness to point out that the *New York Times* had in years past been editorially horrified at the thought of using secret documents.

In all it was a rough time for the press, and even the U.S. Supreme Court's 6-3 verdict in favor of the *New York Times* and the *Washington Post* was hardly the ringingly unanimous decision many editors would have liked.

But an equally disturbing spilt was apparent in the reaction of most papers' readers. A majority wrote to express support for publication of information from the secret documents, but a substantial majority was unhappy—about using the documents, about invading government secrecy, about the problems it caused the Administration.

And in one public opinion poll readers indicated that they don't really trust the press much more than the government, and aren't ready to sacrifice everything in the interests of a free press.

The controversy—involving grave issues of constitutional rights and the nation's security, and powerful, institutions on both sides—was the stuff in which editorialists glory.

The Public's Right to Know

"The immediate issue," said the *Wall Street Journal*, was whether "an American (is) free to speak and publish without prior restraint or censorship. The answers, under the First and Fourteenth Amendments to the Constitution, is a resounding yes."

One issue touched upon by the *Journal* and other papers was how the documents were obtained. "But a charge of theft," the paper said, "suggests that information has the same status as an Army truck or any other piece of government property. It does not.

"Aside from the paper and ink, which could be called property, this is information dealing with the conduct of the public's business. Whether or not the public should have this information is not a question of property but a question of the public's right to information weighed against security consideration."

The *Baltimore Sun* called for "some rule of reason in 'classifying' government information," arguing that the "top secret" label is used more often to hide administrative errors than to protect vital national secrets.

But columnist Victor Lasky turned the *New York Times*' own words back on itself. Lasky recalled a December, 1962, editorial that attacked the *Saturday Evening Post* for revealing actions of the National Security Council during the Cuban [missile] crisis six weeks before.

In an editorial titled "Breach of Security" the *New York Times* intoned, "How can advisers to the President be expected to give advice freely and easily and at all times honestly and with complete integrity if they have to worry about what their arguments will look like in print a few weeks later?"

But if Lasky was saying the *New York Times* had changed its tune, what would he have said of the Jackson (Miss.) *Clarion-Ledger*?

The *Clarion-Ledger*, politically conservative, has no love lost for the *New York Times*. The newspaper went out of its way in an editorial to recall a *New York Times* series "that depicted Fidel Castro as a sort of Robin Hood bent on agrarian reform." The *Clarion-Ledger* also criticized the decision to publish the Pentagon Papers.

A Two-Sided Issue

"Having said all that," the paper concluded, "we believe the government move to suppress the publication was a mistake ... The right of the people of the nation to know what newspapers can turn up is indisputable."

Another conservative made very uncomfortable by the flap was William Loeb, publisher of the Manchester, N.H., *Union-Leader*. In a front-page editorial, in bold face type, Loeb wrote:

"This newspaper finds it difficult to determine who presents the more disgusting sight, the leftwing newspapers and the leftwing political leaders in the United States who seem determined to vilify their own nation, their own flag, even their armed forces, or the Nixon Administration on the other hand, which is so inept and stupid in its presentation to the American people of what is actually a very good case for the Vietnam war."

Obviously, not all the press was ready to back the *New York Times*. The Birmingham, Ala., *News* said, "Whether or not the thief who took (the papers) and the newspaper editors and the peace-at-any-price activists who read them consider their publication dangerous to the national interest, the person who stamped them top secret had reason to do so.

"So long as that stamp was on them, the theft was a violation of the law and the publication, however rationalized, was the height of irresponsibility."

The *Detroit News* said flatly that it "does not agree with those of our press colleagues contending that national interest—and the cause of a free press—are served by the current battle over publication of secret Pentagon papers."

At its extreme, the paper said, the practice would allow publication of secret weapon plans and intelligence reports, which "would result in a disastrous (for the press) collision between press freedom and the manifest democratic need for orderly government."

The editors added that the *News* "does not want the freedom of press so important to our existence stretched to justify this type of irresponsibility."

Voice of the People

Meanwhile, the readers were also reacting. Their verdict was generally favorable to what the *New York Times*, the *Washington Post*, and other papers around the country had done, but some had reservations.

A Connecticut resident wrote to the *New York Times* to say, "The publication of highly classified material from government files in the Vietnam war is in my opinion treason, and it is my hope that you and your associates will be prosecuted to the full extent of the law."

But most letters to the papers which ran the Pentagon Papers stories tended to favor the actions of the press, at least at first. Some papers, including the *Los Angeles Times*, found that the percentage of critical letters tended to pick up after a few days, although remaining a minority. A count of one stack of letters found 34 favorable, 26 against.

Robert Healy, executive editor of the *Boston Globe*, reports the paper received over 200 phone calls the day its Pentagon Papers story appeared, "overwhelmingly favorable." The mail has been the same, Healy adds. "We got a lot of letters from young people thanking us for publishing it."

The *Christian Science Monitor*, also in Boston, surprised some of its readers with a Pentagon Papers story of its own, and editor John Hughes reports that all mail and phone response has been favorable.

The *Chicago Daily News* found that its readers also favored publication. . . .

Mixed Opinion

Newsweek magazine commissioned the Gallup Poll to find out what a representative sampling of Americans thought about the publication of the papers.

Gallup reported 48% of the people polled said they disapproved of government attempts to keep the paper from publishing; 33% favored the government and 19% had no opinion. Yet, an almost identical plurality felt that there was greater harm done to national security by publishing the documents than to freedom of the press by the attempts to block publication.

A majority—56%—felt that the government keeps too much information secret, but the same percentage felt the press is too quick to print classified material whether or not it might hurt national security.

In short, the poll indicates that the public is hardly foursquare behind what the *New York Times* and other papers did, and most are just as dubious about the judgment of the government.

And then, of course, there are those people who have no opinion at all. In the *Newsweek* poll they ranged from 12% to 19% of the total—up to one adult in five.

The *Montana Standard* in Butte ran wire service stories on the Pentagon Papers, editorials, columns and cartoons. Yet Jeffrey Gibson, editor of the editorial page, reports he hasn't received a single letter from a reader on the controversy.

"In my experience there is damned little reaction in this community to anything that happens outside Butte," Gibson says.

*"The Pentagon Papers did contain some
information that could have inflicted
some injury."*

A Reevaluation of *New York Times v. United States*

David Rudenstine

*The following selection is excerpted from the introduction to
David Rudenstine's 1996 book* The Day the Presses Stopped: A
History of the Pentagon Papers Case. *Rudenstine explains that
in 1971, as the case made its way to the Supreme Court, he believed that the Nixon White House had sued the* New York
Times *and* Washington Post *in order to squelch the Pentagon
Papers for the sole purpose of avoiding embarrassment. Years
later, after conducting his own independent research, he came to
believe that Justice Department officials sincerely thought that
disseminating the papers was a legitimate threat to national security and that a halt in publication would allow sufficient time
to accurately measure their impact. Moreover, while he agrees
with the Court's decision allowing the papers to be published,
Rudenstine contends that the documents did contain information that could have harmed the nation's war effort.*

*Rudenstine is a longtime professor of constitutional law at
Yeshiva University's Benjamin N. Cardozo School of Law. In
2001 he was appointed the school's dean.*

At the time [of *New York Times v. United States* (1971)] it
was my belief that the government was merely trying to
suppress information that would be politically embarrassing

David Rudenstine, *The Day the Presses Stopped: A History of the Pentagon Papers
Case,* Danvers, MA: University of California Press, 1996. Republished with permission
of University of California Press, conveyed through Copyright Clearance Center, Inc.

and might undermine support for its war policies. I also had the impression from news reports that the government was trying to steamroll its way to a legal victory by having national security officials make dire warnings of what might happen if the government lost. Indeed, I accepted as true what many said at this time—the government did not offer any specific references to the Pentagon Papers to support its allegations that publication of the top secret study would seriously harm national security.

There were several reasons for my skepticism. The Pentagon Papers seemed no more than a history (which was what the government entitled the study) of America's involvement in Vietnam from 1945 to 1968. In addition that is what the *Times* said the documents were: "The documents in question belong to history. They refer to the development of American interest and participation in Indochina from the post–World War II period up to mid-1968, which is now almost three years ago. Their publication could not conceivably damage American security interests, much less the lives of Americans or Indochinese." At the time and under the circumstances of the case I placed more trust in the *Times* than I did in the [Richard M.] Nixon administration. [U.S. District Court for the Southern District of New York] Judge [Murray I.] Gurfein's ultimate ruling against the government seemed to confirm my initial disbelief that continued publication of the remaining Pentagon Papers would injure current military, diplomatic, or intelligence interests. Once the Supreme Court ruled against the government and the newspapers published their reports with no apparent harm to the national security, the evidence seemed overwhelming that the government's lawsuits against the *Times* and the [*Washington*] *Post* were nothing more than an effort at brazen and unwarranted censorship.

Rethinking the Pentagon Papers Case

That remained my view until I decided to obtain some of the basic legal documents in the case in the late 1980s. One of the first I obtained was labeled "Special Appendix," a government document submitted to a federal appeals court in the *Times* case that was sealed during the litigation. It alleged that further publication of the classified material would injure current troop movements, disclose current and important intelligence matters, and harm current diplomatic efforts aimed at ending the war and gaining the release of American prisoners. In support of these allegations it provided numerous specific page references to the Pentagon Papers. This document, along with others, eventually caused me to begin rethinking the meaning of the litigation over the Pentagon Papers, just as many had claimed that the disclosures of the Pentagon Papers themselves had caused them to reconsider the U.S. military intervention in Vietnam.

Reconsidering the Pentagon Papers case was an incremental, uncertain, and complex process. My first expectations were quite limited, but the more I inquired, the more I expanded the scope of my inquiry. Before long I began to focus on why [Defense Secretary Robert] McNamara had originally decided to commission the study, why [Defense Department employee] Daniel Ellsberg had decided to make the papers available to the *Times*, why the *Times* and the *Post* had determined they would publish the papers, and why the Nixon administration sued the newspapers. Suddenly, every aspect of the litigation seemed open to careful review and analysis and less clear-cut than I had originally thought. . . .

The Government's Concerns Were Understandable

The conclusions I eventually reached differed substantially from the conception of the case I once held and from what I think was (and remains) the dominant view of the case. Although I strongly approve—as I did in 1971—of the Supreme Court's decision, I no longer regard the legal dispute as an effort by the Nixon administration merely to withhold deeply embarrassing information. Nor do I understand the legal attack on the *Times* simply as part of the administration's general campaign to intimidate the press or view the case as one in which the ultimate outcome was relatively predictable because it was based on the application of well-settled, concrete, and definite legal principles applied to a situation in which the government's evidence was unequivocally insufficient.

Instead, I think that the Justice Department lawyers, who first determined whether the government should respond to the *Times* series, and the national security officials with whom they consulted accepted that the *Times*'s Pentagon Papers series potentially threatened important national security interests. They urged the administration to sue the *Times* for a prior restraint because it was the only way to gain time to assess the full implications of this massive leak of classified documents and because it was the only effective legal remedy against the *Times*. Moreover, by the time the litigation was reviewed by the Supreme Court, the government had significantly marshaled its evidence and sharpened its allegations. Indeed, it now appears that the Pentagon Papers did contain some information that could have inflicted some injury—at least to a degree that makes the concerns of national security officials understandable—if disclosed, which it was not.

Causes for Concern

For example, the government's sealed brief in the Supreme Court, which contained many references to the Pentagon Papers, claimed that the disclosure of this information would cause "immediate and irreparable harm to the security of the United States." It stressed that making public the recent diplomatic history of the war would likely "close up channels of communication which otherwise would have some opportunity of facilitating the closing of the Vietnam war." It claimed that further disclosures might reduce the rate of American troop withdrawal from Vietnam. It asserted that the top secret documents identified some CIA agents and activities as well as other intelligence operations and assessments. It also alleged that the classified material contained current military plans.

Although the government's references to the Pentagon Papers did not in the end convince the justices on the high court that additional publication would cause immediate and irreparable harm to the national security, that did not mean that further publications would necessarily be totally harmless. There is an enormous difference between concluding that the Pentagon Papers contained absolutely no information that could injure the national security in one respect or another and concluding that it contained information that would result in immediate and irreparable harm. Thus, concluding that the government's evidence fell short of the legal requirements for a prior restraint did not mean the government's overall case was so weak that further disclosures did not threaten national security.

I also think that prior judicial decisions did not compel the outcome in the case. There was, of course, a wealth of prior cases construing the First Amendment and delineating numerous aspects of freedom of the press. But the Pentagon Papers litigation was the federal government's first effort to enjoin the press because of national security considerations. As a result this was a case of first impression, a lawyer's term meaning that there was no prior judicial decision in a similar case that was directly applicable. This gave the judges substantial discretion in defining the pertinent legal standard. In fact the judges had such discretion that they could have enjoined the newspapers from publishing the Pentagon reports without overruling even one prior decision.

Setting New Standards

Thus, prior case law left unresolved several highly important questions as to what the government had to prove to win a prior restraint. For example, precisely what kind of injury to the national security did the government have to prove to win? Would it be sufficient for the government merely to prove that additional disclosures of classified information would possibly injure diplomatic efforts aimed at securing a peace settlement? Or would the government have to prove that additional reports might reveal information that would endanger the lives of one, ten, or one hundred soldiers? Or would the government have to prove that public disclosure would inflict some irreparable and profound blow to the overall security of the nation?

Prior judicial decisions also left undefined what the government had to prove with regard to the quickness and directness with which a disclosure would cause the feared injury. Thus, would it be enough for the government merely to prove that the disclosure would cause the threatened injury at some indefinite time in the future? Or would the government have to prove that the harm to the nation's security would follow almost immediately and directly after publication? Furthermore, how likely must it be that the publication would cause injury? Would it be sufficient if the government only proved it was possible that publication would injure national security? Or would the government have to prove it was highly likely, if not a virtual certainty, that disclosure would inflict injury? Or were the relevant considerations so complicated that no simple formulation of a legal standard was possible?

Because prior decisions did not answer these questions, the outcome in the Pentagon Papers case was hardly a foregone conclusion. Indeed, the Supreme Court could have decided the Pentagon Papers case either way—for the press or for the government—without straying beyond the parameters defined by prior case law.

A Matter of Exceptional Importance

Moreover, the difficulty of the case—and ultimately its full significance—cannot be fully appreciated without recognizing that the nation was at war when the government tried to suppress these documents marked top secret. Another day's installment of the Pentagon Papers would endanger military, diplomatic, and intelligence matters, the government claimed; it asserted that in cases involving national security the courts had an obligation to defer to the executive branch; and it maintained that the judges lacked the training, information, and experience to make sound judgments when national security matters were in dispute.

Nonetheless, the newspapers prevailed. The fact that they did in the midst of all these circumstances makes their triumph a matter of exceptional importance not only for the freedom of the American press but for American democracy as a whole.

> *"The issues raised by the 1971 publication and its aftermath—presidential power, the role of the courts and the press, government secrecy—are all still with us."*

The Lessons of *New York Times v. United States* Have Faded

Anthony Lewis

In this analysis, written over three decades after the Supreme Court's ruling in New York Times v. United States, *Anthony Lewis examines the immediate and long-term impact of the case. In the short term, the publication of the Pentagon Papers led to a reexamination of the boundaries of presidential power. The Court's involvement reflected the notion that American foreign policy was not the sole domain of the executive branch of government. By choosing to publish the papers, the* Times *and other newspapers reaffirmed the role of the press in America to question government policies rather than merely convey them to readers. Lewis contends that in the decades following the decision the press has retreated from its role as a government watchdog, while the executive branch has assumed greater power. Only the courts, he argues, have taken action to keep a tight rein on presidential power in a manner consistent with the legacy of* New York Times v. United States.

> *This excerpt is from a review of* Inside the Pentagon Papers, *edited by John Prados and Margaret Pratt Porter and published*

in 2005. Lewis, its author, is a former Pulitzer prize–winning New York Times *reporter and editorial columnist.*

It was June 13, 1971, when *The New York Times* began publishing long articles on, and excerpts from, what came to be known as the Pentagon Papers: a secret history of the Vietnam War, prepared in the Pentagon. The uproar occasioned by the publication is dim and distant now; even among those who remember it, many probably think the whole episode did not matter much in the end. But it mattered a lot.

Challenging the Core of Presidential Power

Presidential power was one thing affected by the publication and the controversy that followed. President [Richard] Nixon saw what the *Times* and then other newspapers did as a challenge to his authority. In an affidavit in 1975 he said the Pentagon Papers were "no skin off my back"—because they stopped their history in 1968, before he took office. But, he said, "the way I saw it was that far more important than who the Pentagon Papers reflected on, as to how we got into Vietnam, was the office of the Presidency of the United States. . . ."

Nixon ordered his lawyers to go to court to stop the *Times* from continuing to publish its Pentagon Papers series. Then, angry because [FBI director] J. Edgar Hoover was less than enthusiastic about acting against possible sources of the leaked documents, especially Daniel Ellsberg, Nixon created the White House unit known as the Plumbers. They arranged a break-in at the office of Ellsberg's psychiatrist to get his records. (They also discussed, but did not carry out, the idea of fire-bombing the Brookings Institution in Washington and sending in agents dressed as firemen to look for connections to the leak.) The lawlessness of the Plumbers, and the presidential state of mind they reflected, led to Watergate and Nixon's resignation in 1974. One lesson of those years was seen to be that presidents are not above the law.

Public disclosure of the Pentagon Papers challenged the core of a president's power: his role in foreign and national security affairs. Throughout the cold war, until well into the Vietnam era, virtually all of the public had been content to let presidents—of both parties—make that policy. As the Vietnam War ground on, cruelly and fruitlessly, dissent became significant. The Pentagon Papers showed us that there had all along been dissent inside the government. Thomas Powers, in an essay in *Inside the Pentagon Papers*, says that their disclosure "broke a kind of spell in this country, a notion that the people and the government had to always be in consensus on all the major [foreign policy] issues."

The Courts and the Press

The courts were another institution changed by the Pentagon Papers. Judges tend to defer to executive officials on issues of national security, explaining that they themselves lack necessary expertise. But here, in a case involving thousands of pages of top secret documents, they said no to hyperbolic government claims of damage that would be done if the newspapers were allowed to go on publishing—soldiers' lives lost, alliances damaged. The government's request for an injunction against publication was turned down by a federal trial judge in New York, by a trial judge and the Court of Appeals in Washington in the *Washington Post* case, and finally by the Supreme Court. Floyd Abrams, one of the assisting lawyers who went on from the *Times* case to become a leading First Amendment lawyer, has said that "the enduring lesson of the Pentagon Papers case . . . is the need for the greatest caution and dubiety by the judiciary in accepting representations by the government as to the likelihood of harm."

The press was also profoundly affected by the Pentagon Papers. In the Washington of the 1950s and 1960s, correspondents and columnists shared the government's premises on the great issues of foreign policy, notably the cold war. The press believed in the good faith of officials and their superior knowledge. The Vietnam War undermined both those beliefs. The young correspondents in the field, David Halberstam and the rest, knew more about what was happening and reported it more honestly than generals and presidents. But would an establishment newspaper like the *Times* go so far as to publish thousands of pages from top secret documents about the war?

Professors Harold Edgar and Benno Schmidt Jr. of the Columbia Law School wrote that publication of the papers symbolized

> the passing of an era in which newsmen could be counted upon to work within reasonably well understood boundaries in disclosing information that politicians deemed sensitive.

There had been, they said, a "symbiotic relationship between politicians and the press." But

> *The New York Times*, by publishing the papers ... demonstrated that much of the press was no longer willing to be merely an occasionally critical associate devoted to common aims, but intended to become an adversary threatening to discredit not only political dogma but also the motives of the nation's leaders. ...

Lessons of the Pentagon Papers Unlearned

The issues raised by the 1971 publication and its aftermath—presidential power, the role of the courts and the press, government secrecy—are all still with us. ...

The effects that the Pentagon Papers controversy had on some institutions in our society seem to have worn off.

The press, for one, has retreated from the boldness it showed in 1971. *The New York Times* and *The Washington Post* have apologized for having failed adequately to examine the government's claims in the run-up to the Iraq war [that began in 2003]. The press was slow to give serious coverage to the [George W.] Bush administration's assaults on civil liberty, such as the claim that the President can imprison American citizens indefinitely as alleged "enemy combatants" without trial or access to counsel. (Newspapers have more recently emerged from their torpor, for example in vigorously reporting the widespread torture of prisoners held by the US in Iraq, Guantánamo, and Afghanistan, and the Bush administration's legal memoranda that opened the way to torture. Even there, though, some of the breakthrough reporting came from Seymour Hersh and Jane Mayer in *The New Yorker*.)

The crucial lesson of the Pentagon Papers and then Watergate was that presidents are not above the law. So we thought. But today [in 2005] government lawyers argue that the president *is* above the law—that he can order the torture of prisoners even though treaties and a federal law forbid it. John Yoo, a former Justice Department official who wrote some of the broad claims of presidential power in memoranda, told Jane Mayer recently that Congress does not have power to "tie the president's hands in regard to torture as an interrogation technique." The constitutional remedy for presidential abuse of his authority, he said, is impeachment. Yoo also told Ms. Mayer that the 2004 [U.S. presidential] election was a "referendum" on the torture issue: the people had spoken, and the debate was over. And so, in the view of this prominent conservative legal thinker, a professor at the University of California law school in Berkeley, an election in which the torture issue was not discussed has legitimized President Bush's right to order its use.

The notion that we have a plebiscitary democracy in this country would have astonished James Madison and the other Framers of the Constitution, who thought they were establishing a federal republic of limited powers. So would the idea that the president can ignore laws passed by Congress. One of the fundamental constitutional checks against abuse of power, as the Framers saw it, was the separation of powers in three branches of the federal government: executive, legislative, judicial. If one overreached, they thought, another would curb its abuse.

Congress as an institution has hardly exercised its checking power since the terrorist attacks of September 11, 2001. It gave President Bush greatly expanded investigative and prosecutorial authority in the Patriot Act. It has only intermittently challenged the unprecedented secrecy he has imposed on government activity.

Some Hope in the Courts

That leaves the third branch, the courts. In the context of the "war on terrorism," would they decide a case like the Pentagon Papers the same way today? No one can be sure. But lately there have been signs that judges are unwilling to be cowed by the claims, made since September 11, of unreviewable presidential power. The Supreme Court ruled last year [2004] that citizens held without trial as "enemy combatants" must have an opportunity to answer official suspicions, and held that prisoners at Guantánamo Bay may file petitions in federal courts for release on habeas corpus.

The Supreme Court made its decision on citizens held without trial in the case of Yaser Esam Hamdi. Rather than tell him its reasons for holding him and letting him answer, the government sent Hamdi back to his home in Saudi Arabia. Then . . . a federal district judge in South Carolina ordered the release of the other American held as an "enemy combatant," Jose Padilla. The judge—Henry F. Floyd, nominated by President Bush in 2003—said: "The court finds that the president has no power, neither express nor implied, neither constitutional nor statutory, to hold petitioner as an enemy combatant." To allow that, Judge Floyd said,

> would not only offend the rule of law and violate this country's tradition, but it would also be a betrayal of this

nation's commitment to the separation of powers that safeguards our democratic values and individual liberties.

It was only a trial judge speaking, and officials immediately said they would appeal. His decision affected one American citizen while mistreatment of prisoners overseas during interrogation, as FBI reports among other things have shown, remains inadequately investigated, much less forbidden. But that a trial judge reached those conclusions, and had the courage to express them, meant something. Perhaps, in the courts, the spirit of the Pentagon Papers lives.

CHAPTER 4

Requiring Reporters to Divulge Their Sources

Chapter Preface

Case Overview: *Branzburg v. Hayes (1972)* In 1969

Paul M. Branzburg, a *Louisville Courier-Journal* reporter, researched an account of two Kentucky men who were preparing to produce and sell hashish, an illegal drug. During the course of his investigation, Branzburg interviewed both men, who provided him with information for his story. They agreed to participate only on condition that their names not appear in print. In the article, which was headlined "The Hash They Make Isn't to Eat" and published on November 15, both men remained anonymous. Branzburg referred to them as "Jack" and "Larry," which were fictitious names.

After his article ran in the *Courier-Journal*, Branzburg was subpoenaed by the Jefferson County district attorney to testify before a grand jury probing drug trafficking in the area. He appeared in court but declined to give evidence, claiming that the First Amendment's guarantee of freedom of the press allows journalists the right to maintain the confidentiality of their sources. Branzburg did not alter his stance upon being cited for contempt of court and ordered to testify by J. Miles Pound, a Kentucky trial court judge. He was subpoenaed a second time, in relation to an article he authored on drug use in Frankfort, Kentucky, but again refused to name his sources. After the state's courts rebuffed Branzburg's request to nullify Pound's order, the journalist requested that the U.S. Supreme Court consider the case. (By this time, John J. Hayes had replaced Pound; hence, the case is referred to as *Branzburg v. Hayes.*)

Along with Branzburg's case, the Court agreed to review two other related cases. The first involved *New York Times* reporter Earl Caldwell's unwillingness to testify before a California grand jury about his research into the radical Black Panthers political organization. The second concerned Paul

Pappas, a reporter for WTEV-TV in New Bedford, Massachusetts, who had refused to answer questions about the Panthers before a state grand jury.

The Supreme Court ruling was announced on June 29, 1972. In a five-to-four decision, it decreed that if a reporter has uncovered information that a grand jury believes is significant, that reporter may be subpoenaed. Furthermore, if subpoenaed, the reporter must reveal the requested information. The reporter cannot refuse to testify on the grounds that doing so would compromise his or her sources. The Court decreed that the right of refusal to testify was not protected by the First Amendment. In such cases, journalists are no different from ordinary citizens. If they refuse to testify, they may be cited for contempt of court and suffer sanctions—including imprisonment.

The Court's decision was controversial and generated substantial public deliberation. In his opinion, Justice Byron R. White indicated that state legislatures could enact laws that shield journalists from grand jury inquiries. His proposition resulted in the passage of legislation by a number of states to protect journalists in these situations.

The *Branzburg v. Hayes* decision impacted heavily on related cases. In 1991 in *Cohen v. Cowles Media Co.*, the Supreme Court decreed that the First Amendment does not safeguard reporters from being sued by informants whose identities are divulged without their permission. In 2005 *Branzburg v. Hayes* was tested when *New York Times* and *Time* magazine reporters Judith Miller and Matthew Cooper were threatened with imprisonment. Both refused to reveal the identities of their confidential sources in a grand jury probe into the disclosure to the press of an undercover CIA agent, a federal crime. In July, Cooper avoided incarceration by agreeing to testify—but only after his source authorized the release of his identity. Miller was jailed from July through October, at which point her source also agreed to allow her to cite him.

> *"Newsmen are not exempt from the normal duty of appearing before a grand jury and answering questions relevant to a criminal investigation."*

The Court's Decision: Reporters Must Divulge Their Sources to Grand Juries

Byron R. White

Branzburg v. Hayes, *which the U.S. Supreme Court heard in 1972, involved three journalists—Paul M. Branzburg, Paul Pappas, and Earl Caldwell—who claimed the right to refuse to reveal their confidential sources while testifying before state grand juries. In a five-to-four ruling, the Court declared that the journalists were required to answer all questions put to them.*

In this excerpt from the majority opinion, Byron R. White states that the Court does not wish to restrain the press in its pursuit of news stories. However, the issue at hand is unrelated to the First Amendment's guarantee of press freedom. Journalists—along with all other citizens—must fully respond to all grand jury questions. This requirement places no burden on their freedom to gather and report information.

White, a Colorado native, former college and professional football player, and Yale Law School graduate, was named to the Supreme Court in 1962. He retired from the Court in 1993 and died nine years later.

Byron R. White, majority opinion, *Branzburg v. Hayes*, 1972.

The issue in these cases is whether requiring newsmen to appear and testify before state or federal grand juries abridges the freedom of speech and press guaranteed by the First Amendment. We hold that it does not. . . .

The Reporters Case

Petitioners [Paul M.] Branzburg and [Paul] Pappas and respondent [Earl] Caldwell press First Amendment claims that may be simply put: that, to gather news, it is often necessary to agree either not to identify the source of information published or to publish only part of the facts revealed, or both; that, if the reporter is nevertheless forced to reveal these confidences to a grand jury, the source so identified and other confidential sources of other reporters will be measurably deterred from furnishing publishable information, all to the detriment of the free flow of information protected by the First Amendment. Although the newsmen in these cases do not claim an absolute privilege against official interrogation in all circumstances, they assert that the reporter should not be forced either to appear or to testify before a grand jury or at trial until and unless sufficient grounds are shown for believing that the reporter possesses information relevant to a crime the grand jury is investigating, that the information the reporter has is unavailable from other sources, and that the need for the information is sufficiently compelling to override the claimed invasion of First Amendment interests occasioned by the disclosure. Principally relied upon are prior cases emphasizing the importance of the First Amendment guarantees to individual development and to our system of representative government, decisions requiring that official action with adverse impact on First Amendment rights be justified by a public interest that is "compelling" or "paramount," and those precedents establishing the principle that justifiable governmental goals may not be achieved by unduly broad means having an unnecessary impact on protected rights of speech, press, or association.

The heart of the claim is that the burden on news gathering resulting from compelling reporters to disclose confidential information outweighs any public interest in obtaining the information.

Not a Free Press Issue

We do not question the significance of free speech, press, or assembly to the country's welfare. Nor is it suggested that news gathering does not qualify for First Amendment protection; without some protection for seeking out the news, freedom of the press could be eviscerated. But these cases involve no intrusions upon speech or assembly, no prior restraint or restriction on what the press may publish, and no express or implied command that the press publish what it prefers to withhold. No exaction or tax for the privilege of publishing, and no penalty, civil or criminal, related to the content of published material is at issue here. The use of confidential sources by the press is not forbidden or restricted; reporters remain free to seek news from any source by means within the law. No attempt is made to require the press to publish its sources of information or indiscriminately to disclose them on request.

The sole issue before us is the obligation of reporters to respond to grand jury subpoenas as other citizens do, and to answer questions relevant to an investigation into the commission of crime. Citizens generally are not constitutionally immune from grand jury subpoenas, and neither the First Amendment nor any other constitutional provision protects the average citizen from disclosing to a grand jury information that he has received in confidence. The claim is, however, that reporters are exempt from these obligations because, if forced to respond to subpoenas and identify their sources or disclose other confidences, their informants will refuse or be reluctant to furnish newsworthy information in the future.

This asserted burden on news gathering is said to make compelled testimony from newsmen constitutionally suspect, and to require a privileged position for them.

Previous Cases Limiting the Press

It is clear that the First Amendment does not invalidate every incidental burdening of the press that may result from the enforcement of civil or criminal statutes of general applicability. Under prior cases, otherwise valid laws serving substantial public interests may be enforced against the press as against others, despite the possible burden that may be imposed. The Court has emphasized that

> [t]he publisher of a newspaper has no special immunity from the application of general laws. He has no special privilege to invade the rights and liberties of others. [*Associated Press v. National Labor Relations Board*, (1937).]

It was there held that the Associated Press, a news-gathering and disseminating organization, was not exempt from the requirements of the National Labor Relations Act. The holding was reaffirmed in *Oklahoma Press Publishing Co. v. Walling* (1946), where the Court rejected the claim that applying the Fair Labor Standards Act to a newspaper publishing business would abridge the freedom of press guaranteed by the First Amendment. . . . *Associated Press v. United States* (1945) similarly overruled assertions that the First Amendment precluded application of the Sherman Act to a news-gathering and disseminating organization. . . .

The prevailing view is that the press is not free to publish with impunity everything and anything it desires to publish. Although it may deter or regulate what is said or published, the press may not circulate knowing or reckless falsehoods damaging to private reputation without subjecting itself to liability for damages, including punitive damages, or even criminal prosecution. A newspaper or a journalist may also be punished for contempt of court, in appropriate circumstances.

Limits on Press Access Are Constitutional

It has generally been held that the First Amendment does not guarantee the press a constitutional right of special access to information not available to the public generally. . . . In *Zemel v. Rusk* [1965], for example, the Court sustained the Government's refusal to validate passports to Cuba even though that restriction "render[ed] less than wholly free the flow of information concerning that country." The ban on travel was held constitutional, for "[t]he right to speak and publish does not carry with it the unrestrained right to gather information."

Despite the fact that news gathering may be hampered, the press is regularly excluded from grand jury proceedings, our own [Supreme Court] conferences, the meetings of other official bodies gathered in executive session, and the meetings of private organizations. Newsmen have no constitutional right of access to the scenes of crime or disaster when the general public is excluded, and they may be prohibited from attending or publishing information about trials if such restrictions are necessary to assure a defendant a fair trial before an impartial tribunal. In *Sheppard v. Maxwell* (1966), for example, the Court reversed a state court conviction where the trial court failed to adopt "stricter rules governing the use of the courtroom by newsmen, as Sheppard's counsel requested," neglected to insulate witnesses from the press, and made no "effort to control the release of leads, information, and gossip to the press by police officers, witnesses, and the counsel for both sides." . . .

It is thus not surprising that the great weight of authority is that newsmen are not exempt from the normal duty of appearing before a grand jury and answering questions relevant to a criminal investigation. At common law, courts consistently refused to recognize the existence of any privilege authorizing a newsman to refuse to reveal confidential information to a grand jury. [In *Garland v. Tate* (1958)], a news gatherer asserted for the first time that the First Amendment exempted confidential information from public disclosure pursuant to a subpoena issued in a civil suit, but the claim was denied, and this argument has been almost uniformly rejected since then. . . .

The Role of a Grand Jury

The prevailing constitutional view of the newsman's privilege is very much rooted in the ancient role of the grand jury that has the dual function of determining if there is probable cause to believe that a crime has been committed and of protecting citizens against unfounded criminal prosecutions. Grand jury proceedings are constitutionally mandated for the institution of federal criminal prosecutions for capital or other serious crimes, and "its constitutional prerogatives are rooted in long centuries of Anglo-American history." [*Hannah v. Larche* (1960).] The Fifth Amendment provides that "[n]o person shall be held to answer for a capital, or otherwise infamous crime, unless on a presentment or indictment of a Grand Jury." The adoption of the grand jury "in our Constitution as the sole method for preferring charges in serious criminal cases shows the high place it held as an instrument of justice." [*Costello v. United States* (1956).] Although state systems of criminal procedure differ greatly among themselves, the grand jury is similarly guaranteed by many state constitutions and plays an important role in fair and effective law enforcement in the overwhelming majority of the States. Because its task is to inquire into the existence of possible criminal conduct and to return only well founded indictments, its investigative powers are necessarily broad.

> It is a grand inquest, a body with powers of investigation and inquisition, the scope of whose inquiries is not to be limited narrowly by questions of propriety or forecasts of

> the probable result of the investigation, or by doubts
> whether any particular individual will be found properly
> subject to an accusation of crime. [*Blair v. United States*
> (1919).]

Hence, the grand jury's authority to subpoena witnesses is not only historic, but essential to its task. Although the powers of the grand jury are not unlimited and are subject to the supervision of a judge, the long-standing principle that "the public ... has a right to every man's evidence," except for those persons protected by a constitutional, common law, or statutory privilege [as stated in *United States v. Bryan*] is particularly applicable to grand jury proceedings.

No Special Privilege

A number of States have provided newsmen a statutory privilege of varying breadth, but the majority have not done so, and none has been provided by federal statute. Until now, the only testimonial privilege for unofficial witnesses that is rooted in the Federal Constitution is the Fifth Amendment privilege against compelled self-incrimination. We are asked to create another by interpreting the First Amendment to grant newsmen a testimonial privilege that other citizens do not enjoy. This we decline to do. Fair and effective law enforcement aimed at providing security for the person and property of the individual is a fundamental function of government, and the grand jury plays an important, constitutionally mandated role in this process. On the records now before us, we perceive no basis for holding that the public interest in law enforcement and in ensuring effective grand jury proceedings is insufficient to override the consequential, but uncertain, burden on news gathering that is said to result from insisting that reporters, like other citizens, respond to relevant questions put to them in the course of a valid grand jury investigation or criminal trial.

This conclusion itself involves no restraint on what newspapers may publish or on the type or quality of information reporters may seek to acquire, nor does it threaten the vast bulk of confidential relationships between reporters and their sources. Grand juries address themselves to the issues of whether crimes have been committed and who committed them. Only where news sources themselves are implicated in crime or possess information relevant to the grand jury's task need they or the reporter be concerned about grand jury subpoenas. Nothing before us indicates that a large number or percentage of all confidential news sources falls into either category and would in any way be deterred by our holding that the Constitution does not, as it never has, exempt the newsman from performing the citizen's normal duty of appearing and furnishing information relevant to the grand jury's task.

Crimes Should Be Punished

The preference for anonymity of those confidential informants involved in actual criminal conduct is presumably a product of their desire to escape criminal prosecution, and this preference, while understandable, is hardly deserving of constitutional protection. It would be frivolous to assert—and no one does in these cases—that the First Amendment, in the interest of securing news or otherwise, confers a license on either the reporter or his news sources to violate valid criminal laws. Although stealing documents or private wiretapping could provide newsworthy information, neither reporter nor source is immune from conviction for such conduct, whatever the impact on the flow of news. Neither is immune, on First Amendment grounds, from testifying against the other, before the grand jury or at a criminal trial. The Amendment does not reach so far as to override the interest of the public in ensuring that neither reporter nor source is invading the rights of other citizens through reprehensible conduct forbidden to all other persons. To assert the contrary proposition is to answer it, since it involves in its very statement the contention that the freedom of the press is the freedom to do wrong with impunity and implies the right to frustrate and defeat the discharge of those governmental duties upon the performance of which the freedom of all, including that of the press, depends. . . . It suffices to say that, however complete is the right of the press to state public things and discuss them, that right, as every other right enjoyed in human society, is subject to the restraints which separate right from wrongdoing. [*Toledo Newspaper Co. v. United States* (1918).]

Thus, we cannot seriously entertain the notion that the First Amendment protects a newsman's agreement to conceal the criminal conduct of his source, or evidence thereof, on the theory that it is better to write about crime than to do something about it. Insofar as any reporter in these cases undertook not to reveal or testify about the crime he witnessed, his claim of privilege under the First Amendment presents no substantial question. The crimes of news sources are no less reprehensible and threatening to the public interest when witnessed by a reporter than when they are not.

> *"I see no way of making mandatory the disclosure of a reporter's confidential source of the information on which he bases his news story."*

Dissenting Opinion: Reporters Should Not Be Required to Divulge Their Sources

William O. Douglas

Four U.S. Supreme Court justices—William O. Douglas, Potter Stewart, William J. Brennan Jr., and Thurgood Marshall—disagreed with the majority opinion in Branzburg v. Hayes. *The 1972 case centered on three journalists—Paul M. Branzburg, Paul Pappas, and Earl Caldwell—who had maintained the right to decline to divulge their confidential sources while testifying before state grand juries. The majority ruled that journalists must answer all questions put to them in such situations.*

This excerpt from the dissenting opinion, written by Douglas, maintains that reporters are protected by the First Amendment from testimony unless they are directly involved in the commission of criminal acts. Furthermore, journalists who choose to testify may invoke their First Amendment rights and refuse to answer individual questions. Spotlighting the case of Caldwell, a reporter for the New York Times, *Douglas notes that if journalists are not granted this protection, grand juries may harass reporters based on their or their papers' political views. This practice would be contrary to the press freedoms guaranteed in the First Amendment and would stifle the free flow of information that is essential in a truly democratic society.*

William O. Douglas, dissenting opinion, *Branzburg v. Hayes*, 1972.

Douglas, a Minnesotan, was known for his independent spirit and aggressive support of individual rights. He was named to the Supreme Court in 1939 and retired in 1975, five years before his death.

It is my view that there is no "compelling need" that can be shown which qualifies the reporter's immunity from appearing or testifying before a grand jury, unless the reporter himself is implicated in a crime. His immunity, in my view, is therefore quite complete, for, absent his involvement in a crime, the First Amendment protects him against an appearance before a grand jury, and, if he is involved in a crime, the Fifth Amendment stands as a barrier. ... And since, in my view, a newsman has an absolute right not to appear before a grand jury, it follows for me that a journalist who voluntarily appears before that body may invoke his First Amendment privilege to specific questions. The basic issue is the extent to which the First Amendment ... must yield to the Government's asserted need to know a reporter's unprinted information.

The starting point for decision pretty well marks the range within which the end result lies. The *New York Times*, whose reporting functions are at issue here, takes the amazing position that First Amendment rights are to be balanced against other needs or conveniences of government. My belief is that all of the "balancing" was done by those who wrote the Bill of Rights. By casting the First Amendment in absolute terms, they repudiated the timid, watered-down, emasculated versions of the First Amendment which both the Government and the *New York Times* advance in the case.

The First Amendment Protects the Power of the People over the Government

My view is close to that of the late [philosopher and free speech advocate] Alexander Meiklejohn:

For the understanding of these principles, it is essential to keep clear the crucial difference between "the rights" of the governed and "the powers" of the governors. And at this point, the title "Bill of Rights" is lamentably inaccurate as a designation of the first ten amendments. They are not a "Bill of Rights," but a "Bill of Powers and Rights." The Second through the Ninth Amendments limit the powers of the subordinate agencies in order that due regard shall be paid to the private "rights of the governed." The First and Tenth Amendments protect the governing "powers" of the people from abridgment by the agencies which are established as their servants. In the field of our "rights," each one of us can claim "due process of law." In the field of our governing "powers," the notion of "due process" is irrelevant.

He also believed that

[s]elf-government can exist only insofar as the voters acquire the intelligence, integrity, sensitivity, and generous devotion to the general welfare that, in theory, casting a ballot is assumed to express,

and that

[p]ublic discussions of public issues, together with the spreading of information and opinion bearing on those issues, must have a freedom unabridged by our agents. Though they govern us, we, in a deeper sense, govern them. Over our governing, they have no power. Over their governing, we have sovereign power.

Two principles which follow from this understanding of the First Amendment are at stake here. One is that the people, the ultimate governors, must have absolute freedom of, and therefore privacy of, their individual opinions and beliefs regardless of how suspect or strange they may appear to others. Ancillary to that principle is the conclusion that an individual must also have absolute privacy over whatever information he may generate in the course of testing his opinions and beliefs.

In this regard, [*New York Times* reporter Earl] Caldwell's status as a reporter is less relevant than is his status as a student who affirmatively pursued empirical research to enlarge his own intellectual viewpoint. The second principle is that effective self-government cannot succeed unless the people are immersed in a steady, robust, unimpeded, and uncensored flow of opinion and reporting which are continuously subjected to critique, rebuttal, and reexamination. In this respect, Caldwell's status as a news gatherer and an integral part of that process becomes critical.

The Inviolability of Privacy

Government has many interests that compete with the First Amendment. Congressional investigations determine how existing laws actually operate or whether new laws are needed. While congressional committees have broad powers, they are subject to the restraints of the First Amendment. As we said in *Watkins v. United States* [1957]:

> Clearly, an investigation is subject to the command that the Congress shall make no law abridging freedom of speech or press or assembly. While it is true that there is no statute to be reviewed, and that an investigation is not a law, nevertheless an investigation is part of lawmaking. It is justified solely as an adjunct to the legislative process. The First Amendment may be invoked against infringement of the protected freedoms by law or by lawmaking.

Hence, matters of belief, ideology, religious practices, social philosophy, and the like are beyond the pale and of no rightful concern of government, unless the belief or the speech, or other expression has been translated into action.

Also at stake here is Caldwell's privacy of association. We have held that

> [i]nviolability of privacy in group association may in many circumstances be indispensable to preservation of freedom

of association, particularly where a group espouses dissident beliefs. [*NAACP v. Alabama* [1958]; *NAACP v. Button* [1963].]

As I said in *Gibson v. Florida Legislative Investigation Committee* [1963]:

> the associational rights protected by the First Amendment ... cover the entire spectrum in political ideology as well as in art, in journalism, in teaching, and in religion. ... [G]overnment is ... precluded from probing the intimacies of spiritual and intellectual relationships in the myriad of such societies and groups that exist in this country, *regardless of the legislative purpose sought to be served.* ... If that is not true, I see no barrier to investigation of newspapers, churches, political parties, clubs, societies, unions, and any other association for their political, economic, social, philosophical, or religious views. (emphasis added.)

Disregarding the First Amendment

The Court has not always been consistent in its protection of these First Amendment rights, and has sometimes allowed a government interest to override the absolutes of the First Amendment. For example, under the banner of the "clear and present danger" test, and later under the influence of the "balancing" formula, the Court has permitted men to be penalized not for any harmful conduct, but solely for holding unpopular beliefs.

In recent years, we have said over and over again that, where First Amendment rights are concerned, any regulation "narrowly drawn," must be "compelling," and not merely "rational" as is the case where other activities are concerned. But the "compelling" interest in regulation neither includes paring down or diluting the right nor embraces penalizing one solely for his intellectual viewpoint; it concerns the State's interest, for example, in regulating the time and place or perhaps manner of exercising First Amendment rights. Thus, one has an undoubted right to read and proclaim the First Amendment in the classroom or in a park. But he would not have the right to blare it forth from a sound truck rolling through the village or city at 2 a.m. The distinction drawn in *Cantwell v. Connecticut* (1940) should still stand:

> [T]he Amendment embraces two concepts,—freedom to believe and freedom to act. The first is absolute, but, in the nature of things, the second cannot be.

Under these precedents, there is no doubt that Caldwell could not be brought before the grand jury for the sole purpose of exposing his political beliefs. Yet today the Court effectively permits that result under the guise of allowing an attempt to elicit from him "factual information." To be sure, the inquiry will be couched only in terms of extracting Caldwell's recollection of what was said to him during the interviews, but the fact remains that his questions to the [Black] Panthers [a black radical group], and therefore the respective answers, were guided by Caldwell's own preconceptions and views about the Black Panthers. His entire experience was shaped by his intellectual viewpoint. Unlike the random bystander, those who affirmatively set out to test a hypothesis, as here, have no tidy means of segregating subjective opinion from objective facts.

Sooner or later, any test which provides less than blanket protection to beliefs and associations will be twisted and relaxed so as to provide virtually no protection at all. . . .

Importance of a Free Press

Today's decision will impede the wide-open and robust dissemination of ideas and counterthought which a free press both fosters and protects and which is essential to the success of intelligent self-government. Forcing a reporter before a grand jury will have two retarding effects upon the ear and the pen of the press. Fear of exposure will cause dissidents to communicate less openly to trusted reporters. And fear of accountability will cause editors and critics to write with more restrained pens.

I see no way of making mandatory the disclosure of a reporter's confidential source of the information on which he bases his news story. . . .

A reporter is no better than his source of information. Unless he has a privilege to withhold the identity of his source, he will be the victim of governmental intrigue or aggression. If he can be summoned to testify in secret before a grand jury, his sources will dry up and the attempted exposure, the effort to enlighten the public, will be ended. If what the Court sanctions today becomes settled law, then the reporter's main function in American society will be to pass on to the public the press releases which the various departments of government issue.

It is no answer to reply that the risk that a newsman will divulge one's secrets to the grand jury is no greater than the threat that he will, in any event, inform to the police. Even the most trustworthy reporter may not be able to withstand relentless badgering before a grand jury.

The record in this case is replete with weighty affidavits from responsible newsmen, telling how important is the sanctity of their sources of information. When we deny newsmen that protection, we deprive the people of the information needed to run the affairs of the Nation in an intelligent way.

A Prologue to a Tragedy

[Founding Father James] Madison said:

> A popular Government, without popular information or the means of acquiring it, is but a Prologue to a Farce or a Tragedy, or perhaps both. Knowledge will forever govern ignorance, and a people who mean to be their own Governors, must arm themselves with the power which knowledge gives.

Today's decision is more than a clog upon news gathering. It is a signal to publishers and editors that they should exercise caution in how they use whatever information they can obtain. Without immunity, they may be summoned to account for their criticism.

The intrusion of government into this domain is symptomatic of the disease of this society. As the years pass, the power of government becomes more and more pervasive. It is a power to suffocate both people and causes. Those in power, whatever their politics, want only to perpetuate it. Now that the fences of the law and the tradition that has protected the press are broken down, the people are the victims. The First Amendment, as I read it, was designed precisely to prevent that tragedy.

> *"We must make certain we protect the right of the individual and of the media to dissent in a lawful way."*

Shield Laws Are Needed to Protect the Press

Herbert G. Klein

On June 29, 1972, the U.S. Supreme Court delivered its opinion on Branzburg v. Hayes, *with the majority ruling that reporters must answer all questions put to them by grand juries. On September 21 the* Washington Post *printed excerpts from a speech delivered by Herbert G. Klein before the Hastings College of the Law in San Francisco. Klein was then serving in the administration of President Richard M. Nixon as director of the Office of Communications.*

In his remarks Klein criticizes the Branzburg case as excessive government regulation of the media. In response, he supports the passage of federal and state "shield laws," which would prevent government agencies from compelling journalists to reveal information obtained during the news-gathering process. Such laws would not hamper law enforcement, he insists, because they would only protect testimony that does not involve specific lawbreaking, cannot be obtained elsewhere, or is not of vital importance to the state of the nation.

Klein served under Nixon from 1969 to 1973. He was editor in chief of the Copley Newspapers from 1980 to 2003.

Herbert G. Klein, "A White House Aide on Control of the Press," *Washington Post*, September 21, 1972, p. A22. Reproduced by permission of the author.

[The *Branzburg v. Hayes*] . . . Supreme Court decision compelling newsmen to divulge information from confidential sources to grand juries has renewed interest in the free press/fair trial controversy.

On the one side is the traditional right of the press to gather and publish news and opinion as it sees fit. On the other is the equally traditional right of the judicial system to obtain any and all evidence needed in carrying out thorough criminal or civil proceedings.

While current law clearly supports the government's position, we must not forget the maxim that "hard cases make bad law." As you know, there are some situations where the public interest is better served by negotiations and self-restraint than by judicial mandate, and where it is in the interests of all concerned to avoid a confrontation and an imposed settlement.

The Department of Justice has historically been cautious in subpoenaing the press. This caution was reflected by former Attorney General John N. Mitchell in February, 1970, when he said he regretted "any implication" that the federal government "is interfering in the traditional freedom and independence of the press." Mr. Mitchell said his policy was to negotiate with the press prior to the issuance of subpoenas, in an effort to maintain a balance with respect to free press/fair trial interests. In August, 1970, the Attorney General issued the first set of departmental guidelines for use by Justice Department attorneys in requesting courts to subpoena the media. The guidelines were met with approval from both the bar and the journalistic societies. . . .

The fundamental purpose of the First Amendment is to enlighten the public. It would seem to follow that if the public has the right to receive information, the press should have the right to disseminate information. But the Supreme Court has never actually recognized the newsman's right to gather news. In the past, decisions by the Court dealt only with the newsman's right to *publish* news. In 1935, the right to gather news was recognized by a Federal Court of Appeals, but the decision was later reversed by the Supreme Court, on grounds other than the First Amendment. Therefore, while the Supreme Court has had dozens of cases involving freedom of expression, it had never before decided a case directly on the question of press subpoenas.

A Wary Media

You can appreciate the uproar that took place . . . when the Supreme Court made its 5-to-4 decision, holding that the First Amendment does not shield a reporter automatically from having to disclose information or sources to a grand jury. Newsmen feared that their confidential sources would hesitate to offer information if they knew there was danger of losing their anonymity. Editors claimed that broad subpoenas would impose heavy administrative requirements on their news departments. Cameramen and reporters said they felt they would be viewed as government agents and subjected to harassment when covering certain public events.

In an effort to counteract these repercussions and continue to protect the confidentiality of their sources and information, five major news organizations joined together to support a proposal entitled the "Free Flow of Information Act." This Joint Media Committee, as it is called, is comprised of the American Society of Newspaper Editors; the Associated Press Managing Editors Association; National Press Photographers Association; Radio Television News Directors Association; and Sigma Delta Chi, professional journalistic society.

. . . Their proposal is intended to provide broad but not unlimited protection to all who gather information for publication or broadcast. It is similar, but not identical to nearly two dozen newsmen's "shield" bills introduced in the 92nd Congress. It states that those who gather such information "shall not be required" to disclose their information or its source to any official federal body.

The proposal, for which the Joint Media Committee began immediately to seek congressional support, further provides that a federal district court may remove the protective "shield" if it finds "clear and convincing evidence" that:

- The writer or broadcaster probably has information relevant to a specific law violation;

- there are no other means of obtaining the necessary information, and

- there is a "compelling and overriding national interest" in making the information available to the investigative body.

Such determinations by a federal district court could be appealed through the federal court system.

Pro–Shield Laws

Eighteen states have already adopted similar "shield" laws providing newsmen with varying degrees of immunity from state or local investigative bodies. I would like to go on record as favoring the shield laws, but I believe there is a real question as to whether the timing is correct to gain passage of an adequate law by the Congress. . . . I would only point out that Congress came within an eyelash of supporting [West Virginia] Congressman [Harley] Staggers' effort to cite for contempt the President of CBS for his refusal to release film outtakes. I oppose further regulation of the media.

I would urge journalistic societies to proceed as rapidly as possible with additional state shield laws in order to provide the media with necessary protection while Congressional action is under study.

If a random group of lawyers had been asked [pre–*Branzburg v. Hayes*] . . . to define the legal rights of newsmen in refusing to testify under subpoena, to protect their sources, the answer from most probably would have been "none." But the highly visual cases of Earl Caldwell of the *New York Times*,

Paul M. Branzburg of the *Louisville Courier-Journal*, and Paul Pappas of WTEV-TV in New Bedford, Massachusetts, have gone a long way in changing this.

Mr. Caldwell and Mr. Pappas were called to testify about black conspirators. Mr. Caldwell was covering the Black Panther party in the San Francisco area. The grand jury called him in to investigate possible threats against the President and the violent overthrow of the government. Mr. Caldwell refused to comply with the subpoena.

Mr. Pappas was allowed to spend a night in Black Panther headquarters in New Bedford during some racial uprisings in 1970. It was agreed that if there were a raid, he would report on police methods; but if there were no raid, he would write nothing. As it turned out, no raid took place and he wrote no report. Later, he was subpoenaed to give information about the Panthers. He refused and was held in contempt.

Mr. Branzburg was subpoenaed after writing articles dealing with the marijuana trade. Mr. Branzburg would not enter the grand jury room, claiming that the First Amendment shielded him from making testimony. The Supreme Court of Kentucky ruled against him and he appealed to the U.S. Supreme Court.

Government-Media Conflict

These incidents illustrate two things: That the government has usually issued subpoenas to the press to obtain information about political conspirators, and that the information being subpoenaed usually went well beyond the *identity* of a confidential source. Both elements are important, but the second is having more impact because it is broadening the area of conflict between the government and press. In so doing, it is making obsolete most of the legislation that has been passed in prior years dealing with this relationship.

In all of these considerations, we must make certain we protect the right of the individual and of the media to dissent in a lawful way.

A traditional part of the American system is a press that is free to criticize. However, I should add that, too often, the press fails to recognize that officials of the government also have the right to be critical of the press. . . .

In a general way, I think we should be looking at what measures are necessary to protect the notes of reporters and the out-takes of film. We should also continue to recognize that newsmen have duties as *citizens*. In this day and age, there is constant danger of over-regulation, particularly as it refers to the broadcast industry. With the introduction of cable and other innovations, which have widened the broadcast spectrum, I believe the time has come to consider *less* regulation, not more.

> *"Taking on the institutional press is
> never good for the Court's own politi-
> cal capital, its own reputation."*

Branzburg Has Been
Applied Inconsistently

Elena Kagan and Frederick Schauer, interview by
Robb London

*In the following selection, written thirty-three years after the
U.S. Supreme Court delivered its opinion in* Branzburg v. Hayes,
*Elena Kagan and Frederick Schauer, two distinguished constitu-
tional law experts, discuss why the decision remains at issue.
Specifically, they explore the case as it relates to one of the major
press-related news stories of the first years of the twenty-first
century. In 2003 a columnist cited anonymous government
sources in an article disclosing the identity of Valerie Plame as
an undercover CIA agent. Because it is illegal for government officials to disclose the identity of CIA agents, an investigation was
launched to discover who leaked this sensitive information to the
media. Some of the reporters involved in the case refused to
name their sources when summoned by a grand jury.*

Kagan and Schauer dissect the meaning of Branzburg *in relation to these events. Despite the decision, many journalists still
claim the right to keep their sources confidential, and courts
grant it in some cases. Lawyers have cited* Branzburg *in arguing
that the requirement for journalists to testify can be evaluated
on a case-by-case basis in order to ensure the testimony is actually needed and that the grand jury's intent is not to harass the*

Elena Kagan and Frederick Schauer, interviewed by Robb London, "Faculty View-
points: Can Reporters Refuse to Testify?" *Harvard Law Bulletin*, Spring 2005. © 2005
The President and Felllows of Harvard College. All rights reserved. Reproduced by permission.

reporter. Kagan and Schauer conclude that the meaning of Branzburg *remains unclear.*

After [nationally syndicated] columnist Robert Novak published leaked information in July 2003 revealing that Valerie Plame, the wife of a prominent critic of the [George W.] Bush administration, was a CIA operative, a special prosecutor launched an investigation to determine who was responsible for the leak. When journalists were subpoenaed in federal court, they claimed they were shielded from testifying about confidential sources by the so-called "reporter's privilege." They did so despite the fact that in 1972, in *Branzburg v. Hayes*, the Supreme Court held that no such privilege is available under the First Amendment. In fact, since *Branzburg*, reporters under subpoena have continued to assert the privilege, and many federal courts and more than 30 states still recognize it.

How did this happen? Should the Supreme Court end the confusion by either reiterating *Branzburg's* holding or recognizing a privilege? Should Congress jump in? The [*Harvard Law*] *Bulletin* put these questions to Frederick Schauer . . . , who is the Frank Stanton Professor of the First Amendment at the John F. Kennedy School of Government and a frequent teacher at Harvard Law School, and Dean Elena Kagan . . . , who teaches constitutional law and encountered the reporter's privilege in private practice. The discussion was moderated by Robb London.

Interpreting the Decision

Professor Frederick Schauer: We have to start with *Branzburg v. Hayes*. The 5-4 majority opinion said pretty plainly there is not a privilege. That is, the First Amendment does not command that there be a reporter's privilege. The Supreme Court slightly, but only slightly, qualified that by saying, "Of course, we do not mean to say that when there is no legitimate need for the information, and a subpoena is being used solely for harassment purposes, that the First Amendment does not come into play."

Justice [Lewis F.] Powell [Jr.], who was part of the five, issued his own concurring opinion, saying, in effect, maybe, in order to determine that there's not harassment, there ought to be an investigation in every case to determine whether there is actual need for the information. We don't know what he meant by that. One plausible argument is only that there ought to be an examination in every case to make sure it's not harassment. But the other understanding of it is that it requires a determination of necessity in every case.

Picking up on that fragment in Powell's concurring opinion, lawyers for reporters have had remarkable success convincing a large number of state and federal courts that there needs to be this case-by-case inquiry into necessity, and the Supreme Court has never revisited the issue since *Branzburg*.

Dean Elena Kagan: When I was a lawyer, in my first job after clerking, I worked for Williams & Connolly, and we represented the *Washington Post* and other news outlets. And the *Post* reporters found themselves subpoenaed. And we would walk in with this boilerplate motion to quash these subpoenas based entirely on Powell's concurring opinion, and it really just hung on this very slender thread. Former *Washington Post* editor Ben Bradlee was once quoted as saying that there's a privilege whether or not the Supreme Court says there is. And that's essentially what we went into court saying. And what was shocking is that sometimes we won notwithstanding that there wasn't a whole lot of law in these motions. The prosecutors would back down often after we convinced them that the reporter didn't know anything or wouldn't say anything particularly useful. Or the judge would rule for us on the ground that there wasn't any necessity for the reporter's testimony. And the client—the reporter—never, ever ended up in jail.

The Power of the Press

Robb London: Isn't something like this what happened with [NBC Washington Bureau Chief] Tim Russert in the Valerie Plame situation—the prosecutor backed off?

Schauer: Yes, and it has happened in a number of different cases. The higher visibility the reporter, or the higher visibility the publication, the more likely it is to happen. Prosecutors don't want to be seen as attacking the press, because in large part the people who write about attacks on the press are the press. We shouldn't forget the old slogan, "Never argue with a fellow who buys ink by the barrel."

Kagan: Quite right. And that's part of what allows media lawyers and their clients to think and talk as if *Branzburg* had come out the other way.

Schauer: In fact, the press may not want to take the issue back to the Supreme Court, because the current understanding, in a large number of lower courts, and in a large number of legislatures, about what *Branzburg* means, or about whether there should be a privilege as a matter of policy, is probably much more press-favorable than what the Supreme Court of the United States in 2005 or 2006 would say if asked the question again.

London: Will the Court now look at the question again?

Schauer: It's a touchy issue for the Court. Even justices who, in their hearts, would agree with the majority in *Branzburg* and want to reinforce it recognize that the Court itself has limited political capital. Taking on the institutional press is never good for the Court's own political capital, its own reputation.

Kagan: It's hard to know whether the Court will re-examine the issue. All these high-profile cases may put pressure on the justices to do so. But one reason the Court may not want to rule again in this area is that the status quo isn't so bad, really. It's hard to think of important prosecutions that have not gone forward because reporters have refused to give information. On the other hand, it's hard to make the argument that freedom of the press has been terribly infringed by the legal regime that's been set up. So it may be that the Supreme Court looks at the status quo and says: "Nothing seems terribly wrong with this. People are ignoring a little bit what we said, but it seems to have results that are not too bad, from either perspective."

Will Congress Act?

London: [Connecticut] Sen. Christopher Dodd has proposed a bill that would essentially codify Justice Powell's concurrence in *Branzburg* and put the burden on the prosecutor to show that the subpoena is the only way of getting the reporter's information, and that it isn't for purposes of harassment. Does the Dodd bill have any chance of being passed in its present form?

Schauer: I think if it is passed, it will be passed in somewhat different form than this. I think it is plausible that Congress might be sympathetic to recognizing some sort of a privilege, and might be sympathetic to a bill that puts the burden on the prosecutor to show why the subpoena is necessary and isn't meant to harass the reporter. I think the area of vulnerability of Dodd's bill is in who gets the privilege. This bill turns out to be not only very strong, but very broad. The institutional press would probably favor a bill that was very strong, but narrower—that is, recognizing, as 31 state statutes do, and as the existing Justice Department guidelines do, a privilege that's held by the traditional institutional press. The mainstream press doesn't necessarily want to see the privilege extended to bloggers and a whole range of other people who would, in the language of the bill, qualify for the privilege simply by having the intent to gather information in order to disseminate that information to the public. I think the institutional press and some of its academic supporters are going to be somewhat hesitant to favor a bill that is so broad, on the theory that the broader it is, the weaker it is likely to become in practice.

Deciding Who's Entitled to Protection

Kagan: I think, Fred, that you've just noted the most important question relating to the reporter's privilege: Who's entitled to claim it? When the privilege started, it was meant to cover the establishment press: the *New York Times*, the *Washington Post*, the major television networks. But as our media have become more diverse and more diffuse, the question of who is a member of the press, and so who gets to claim the privilege, has really come to the fore. Is the blogger entitled to claim it? And if the blogger is, then why not you, and me, and everybody else in the world? And once that happens, there's a real problem for prosecutors seeking to obtain information. So the question of whether you can draw lines in this area, and if so how, is the real question of the privilege.

Schauer: I think there are probably two responses. There have been difficult line-drawing problems even before there were bloggers, in terms of the difference between a reporter and a writer of a book, or a writer of a more occasional publication. The 31 state statutes have drawn lines, and there haven't been enormous problems with this. The fact that it's a fuzzy line doesn't mean that we can't draw it. That's what law does all the time.

And although there are line-drawing problems, we may want to say that there are certain institutions that, as institutions, serve in a concentrated way certain kinds of First Amendment functions. We might say that the job of checking government, the job of exposing government wrongdoing, will be largely concentrated, at least for the time being, in what we can moderately easily recognize as the institutional press. The kinds of press we had 30 years ago—the major news magazines, newspapers, radio stations, radio networks, television networks, television stations and so on—have a particular function to serve in society. And indeed, I wish more often we would draw First Amendment lines that recognize some of these institutional realities. A press-specific reporter's privilege would be a step in this direction.

Kagan: Historically, of course, the Supreme Court really hasn't recognized that kind of reality. It hasn't tried to make distinctions among different kinds of press entities. And there may be strong reasons not to do this. First Amendment law is already very complicated. And if you're asking the Court now to superimpose a whole new set of distinctions on what has already become an unbearable number of complex distinctions, you may end up feeling sorry. There are lots and lots of different kinds of press entities and other speakers. And if each one gets its own First Amendment doctrine, that might be a world we don't want to live in.

Branzburg Should Be Overturned or Modified

Julie Hilden

The Branzburg v. Hayes *case came to the forefront over three decades after its ruling. During a 2005 grand jury investigation, reporters Judith Miller and Matthew Cooper refused to divulge the identities of the confidential sources who fed them informa- tion relating to the public disclosure of the identity of Valerie Plame, an undercover CIA operative. Both journalists were threatened with incarceration. Cooper's source eventually sanc- tioned the release of his name, allowing the reporter to testify— and dodge jail time. Miller, however, was incarcerated for eighty- five days until her source also consented to permit her to name him.*

In this opinion piece, Julie Hilden, a First Amendment law- yer and columnist on the FindLaw.com *Web site, cites examples of journalists being subpoenaed in the Plame case and concludes that* Branzburg v. Hayes *should be overturned or modified. Even though grand jury proceedings are held in secret, leaks occasion- ally occur. Such disclosures result in the public exposure of, and possible legal ramifications for, confidential sources. For this rea- son, individuals wishing to maintain their anonymity might be*

Julie Hilden, "Should Reporters Go to Jail for Protecting Sources from the Valerie Plame Grand Jury? The Unfolding Scandal over Who Revealed the CIA Agent's Iden- tity Raises First Amendment Issues." *FindLaw.com*, August 20, 2004. Copyright © 2004 FindLaw, a Thomson business. This column originally appeared on *FindLaw.com*. Re- produced by permission.

less inclined to speak with journalists. Hilden maintains that their willingness to offer information to the media—particularly if it involves government impropriety—is extremely important in a society that values freedom of speech and of the press. However, while the Branzburg *decision gives unfair advantage to prosecutors, journalists on occasion should be required to divulge their sources. Hilden argues for the implementation of a new test that balances law enforcement versus privacy.*

The scandal over the government leak that revealed the identity of CIA operative Valerie Plame to the media has only grown. Meanwhile, its legal ramifications have grown, too.

The leak itself violated federal criminal laws. . . . Now, the investigation of that leak is testing the Constitution itself—in particular, the First Amendment.

Two journalists, *Time* magazine reporter Matthew Cooper and NBC Washington Bureau Chief Tim Russert, made headlines when they challenged subpoenas issued to them by a special grand jury investigating the leak. But Chief Judge Thomas Hogan of the U.S. District Court for the District of Columbia ruled against them, based on Supreme Court precedent. And he did so even though, according to his opinion, the grand jury may "delve into alleged conversations each reporter had with a confidential source." . . .

Meanwhile, on August 13 [2004], the *New York Times* revealed that the grand jury had also subpoenaed one of its reporters, Judith Miller. The *Times* vowed to fight the subpoena. . . . In addition, it has been reported that Walter Pincus of the *Washington Post* has also been subpoenaed—and the *Post*, too, intends to fight the subpoena. . . .

To make good on their vow, the *Times* and *Post* lawyers would then have to appeal—all the way up to the Supreme Court, if necessary. They could well be joined by other news organizations . . .

After all, according to the *Washington Post*, "two top White House officials called at least six Washington journalists" in what appears to be a campaign to destroy Plame and her husband. Among them was syndicated columnist Robert Novak—who originally printed the leak. . . .

Could such an appeal eventually succeed? Perhaps—but only if the Court can be convinced to overrule, or dramatically modify, a key 1972 First Amendment decision.

Genesis of a Controversy

Before addressing the First Amendment questions raised here, it's worth briefly going over the background of the scandal itself.

On July 6, 2003, the *New York Times* published an article by former U.S. ambassador Joseph Wilson charging that President [George W.] Bush, in his 2003 State of the Union address, had "twisted" intelligence relating to Iraq's purported nuclear program. This weighty charge came in the midst of the scandal surrounding the failure of the Administration to unearth any weapons of mass destruction in Iraq.

A little over a week later, on July 14, Novak published a column identifying Wilson's wife, Valerie Plame, as a CIA agent. He implied that "two senior [Bush] administration officials" were his sources for the information.

Their disclosure may have put Plame's very life in jeopardy—and might also have endangered her CIA contacts. (For this reason, in my view, Novak has gotten far too little flak for his decision to publish—and the same is true for the media outlets that published his column, which included the *Washington Post*.)

After much delay, in December 2003, the Department of Justice finally appointed a special counsel [Patrick Fitzgerald] to investigate the matter. . . . And when the special counsel convened a grand jury, the reporters' subpoenas began to issue.

The *Branzburg v. Hayes* Decision

This brings us to Chief Judge Hogan's decision—holding the subpoenas enforceable even if reporters were required to tell the jury information about confidential sources. His decision was based on the Supreme Court's 1972 ruling in *Branzburg v. Hayes.*

Branzburg held that the First Amendment does not allow reporters to resist a grand jury subpoena. In addition, it suggests that this general rule applies even if it means that appearing before the grand jury would require journalists to reveal confidential sources. In a nutshell, *Branzburg* suggested that there is no place for the First Amendment when it comes to grand jury questions to reporters.

At first blush, this holding might seem reasonable. Grand jury proceedings are secret—and breaches of that secrecy are illegal, and can be sanctioned. So can't reporters reveal sources to grand juries without betraying their confidential sources very much—trading one kind of secrecy for another?

Unfortunately, the answer is no. For one thing, leaks from grand juries, especially in high-profile investigations like this one, do occur.

For another thing, even without a leak, sources' identities may well be betrayed—again, especially in a case like this one. If a particular administration official gets indicted by this grand jury, he or she—and the public—can be pretty sure it's because a reporter gave up his identity (just as the official, ironically, gave up the identity of Valerie Plame.)

A Free Press Issue

And from the point of view of many First Amendment thinkers—though not of the *Branzburg* Court—reporters' need to protect confidential sources is a very big deal indeed. It is intimately related both to the freedom of speech, and the freedom of the press.

After all, the press is supposed to function as the Fourth Estate in our society—the watchdog of the government and other powerful institutions. But without confidential sources, it's hard for it to do that in certain crucial cases.

Confidential sources are typically insiders at these very institutions, or at least persons who are vulnerable to them—and they are reasonably afraid of recriminations if their anonymity is not preserved. If the person known as Deep Throat . . . had thought that [*Washington Post* reporters Bob] Woodward and [Carl] Bernstein would have to give up his anonymity, there might never have been a Watergate investigation.

More broadly, how can the press function as a check on—and watchdog of—the government if it cannot protect confidential government sources when such protection is merited?

Confidential sources can be integral to making sure the press is well-informed on issues crucial to our democracy. And whether the press is well-informed, in turn, affects how informed we all are.

So those who support First Amendment rights ought to care deeply about the protection of confidential sources. They may not maintain that this protection has to be absolute. But they should favor at least making the revelation of sources' identity difficult—not virtually automatic, any time a subpoena is issued.

In other words, the need to protect confidential sources should at least sometimes trump the investigative needs of the grand jury. After all, the grand jury has broad power to subpoena virtually anyone. Shouldn't reporters with confidential sources be last—not first—on the list? Or, if possible, shouldn't they be left off the list entirely?

That leads to a key question: When, exactly, should First Amendment press rights trump the grand jury's need to know?

Branzburg's answer: Virtually never. (The exceedingly rare exception it established is in the event [of] a bogus subpoena with no "legitimate law enforcement purpose.")

Branzburg's view was that reporters' interests don't really count at all when subpoenas are legitimate, because prosecutors' interests in law enforcement always so heavily outweigh the interests of the press.

By ruling that way, the *Branzburg* Court went too far. In effect, it read the First Amendment out of the Constitution.

A Balancing Test

In my opinion, the proper test for whether a reporter must answer a given grand jury question ought to balance law enforcement needs against the need for source confidentiality.

I can imagine a case when a confidential source must be revealed—for instance to prevent great harm. But I can also imagine many cases when a confidential source should be protected—when allowing anonymity in such circumstances will serve a strong social good, and encourage sources to rely on reporters' promises of confidentiality and anonymity in the future.

So I believe a balancing test is the right answer. Perhaps the test could be coupled with what the law calls an "exhaustion" requirement—forcing the grand jury to try to get the information it wants from everyone under the sun except reporters, before it resorts to subpoenaing reporters. (This kind of requirement is often imposed in civil actions—such as libel suits in which reporters rely for their allegedly libelous claims on confidential sources.)

Attorneys for the reporters subpoenaed in the Plame case tried to convince Judge Hogan that *Branzburg* allows just this kind of balancing test. But in a persuasive opinion, Hogan countered that *Branzburg* is much more absolute—and pro-subpoena enforcement—than that. So for such a test to exist, it seems *Branzburg* would have to be overruled—or at least modified, to render its pronouncements less absolute.

Could that happen? It's certainly possible. And it's therefore well worth the *Times*'s and *Post*'s making good on their vow to fight the subpoenas, to take this issue all the way up to the Supreme Court if necessary. . . .

What if the Court did modify or overrule *Branzburg*—and create a balancing test such as the one I have suggested? Ironically, even if the *Times*, with its appeals, were to win this war on behalf of itself and all of the press, it could still lose this one battle. Reporters such as Judith Miller might still have to reveal confidential sources with respect to the Plame grand jury.

Applying the Rule

Consider how the balancing test might play out:

First, let's look at the government's interest in getting the reporters' testimony. There's a real law enforcement need to find out who committed this crime. And it doesn't seem that the perpetrators' identities have been revealed in the discovery the Special Counsel has already received from the White House. So it is likely that only the subpoenaed (or soon-to-be-subpoenaed) reporters know who exposed Plame as a CIA agent.

Second, let's look at the First Amendment interest here. The confidential sources were likely willful perpetrators committing a federal felony—not morally-compelled whistleblowers who violated government secrecy rules along the way. And that's a very important distinction.

We need whistleblowers for the press to function. Deep Throat [who in 2005 was revealed to be W. Mark Felt, a former FBI official]. . . might have broken some laws, or violated attorney-client privilege, to talk to Woodward and Bernstein. But if so, it was to serve the greater social good—revealing corruption at the highest levels.

What we don't need is willful perpetrators like those who seem to have been behind the Plame leak. What social purpose was served by outing a CIA agent? Here, the sources seem to have served not the social good or the functioning of democracy, but a personal vendetta—punishing former Ambassador Wilson by putting his wife in danger. And it's not just Valerie Plame who was placed in jeopardy: It's all those whom she protected in her service as a CIA agent.

The sources' disclosure was the crime here, and that is exactly what is being investigated. The sources didn't report a crime by speaking out—they committed one by talking to reporters. So protecting the disclosure, protects the crime.

Journalists as Accomplices

Meanwhile, it's worth noting, too, that the journalists who published Plame's CIA agent identity may well have committed the same crime as their sources (unless there is a First Amendment exception to the criminal law). Their choice to publish the information also arguably aided and abetted their sources' crimes (again, possibly subject to a First Amendment exception).

With all this criminal activity either marring or virtually replacing the reporter-source relationship, where's the First Amendment value in all this?

Another reason the First Amendment interest here is relatively weak is that instead of confiding in a few trusted reporters—Deep Throat–style—the confidential sources themselves apparently did little to protect their own confidentiality. Indeed, they bandied about their information to what appears to have been at least six separate journalists in their campaign to ruin Plame and her husband.

That's not a confidential source-reporter relationship; it's a broad-scale attack campaign.

For our democracy to work, sources do need to be able to trust reporters. But we don't need to support criminal smear campaigns that may cause great harm to innocent people with the very strongest of First Amendment protections.

So suppose the Court were to overrule *Branzburg*, and endorse and apply a balancing test. For the reasons I've cited the grand jury subpoenas still might be held enforceable. But in that instance, the subpoenas would be enforced then for the right reasons—because a balance had been thoughtfully struck, not just because of *Branzburg*'s knee-jerk assumption that prosecutors should get whatever they want when they are investigating.

For the same reasons I believe the First Amendment claim here is not very strong, if I were a journalist with confidential sources in this case, I wouldn't be doing prison time for this one. The journalists were apparently manipulated into aiding an attack on a CIA agent. Now, will they be manipulated right into jail to protect the attackers? Their sources, by all accounts, are perpetrators—not whistleblowers.

If [journalists] do end up in jail, they may want to mull over, while serving time, whether they are really serving the First Amendment by protecting their sources. They may also want to ask themselves who has really been in the driver's seat here, throughout this scandal and the ensuing investigation: The press, or the source? They also should not call themselves First Amendment martyrs: accomplice is a better word.

Organizations to Contact

Accuracy in Media (AIM)
4455 Connecticut Ave. NW, Suite 330,
   Washington, DC   20008
(202) 364-4401 • fax: (202) 364-4098
e-mail: info@aim.org
Web site: www.aim.org

AIM is a conservative watchdog organization. It researches public complaints on errors of fact made by the news media and requests that the errors be corrected publicly. It publishes the *AIM Report* and a syndicated newspaper column.

American Booksellers Foundation for Free Expression (ABFFE)
139 Fulton St., Suite 302, New York, NY   10038
(212) 587-4025 • fax: (212) 587-2436
e-mail: chris@abffe.com;
Web site: www.abffe.com

The mission of ABFFE is to support and defend the First Amendment and an open exchange of ideas, with an emphasis on the content of books. The organization contests restrictions against free speech and often becomes involved in related court cases.

American Civil Liberties Union (ACLU)
125 Broad St., 18th Floor., New York, NY   10004
(212) 549-2500 • fax: (212) 549-2646
e-mail: infoaclu@aclu.org
Web site: www.aclu.org

The ACLU is a national organization that defends the civil rights guaranteed all Americans in the U.S. Constitution. It adamantly opposes censoring any form of speech and publishes handbooks, public policy reports, project reports, civil liberties books, and pamphlets on a wide variety of issues.

American Journalism Review (AJR)

University of Maryland, 1117 Journalism Bldg.,
  College Park, MD   20742-7111
(301) 405-8803 • fax: (301) 405-8323
e-mail: editor@ajr.umd.edu
Web site: www.ajr.org

The AJR is a magazine that reports on all facets of the media. It explores the manner in which the media cover particular events and examines reporting trends and issues related to journalistic ethics. The magazine is published six times a year by the Philip Merrill College of Journalism at the University of Maryland.

American Library Association (ALA)

50 E. Huron St., Chicago, IL   60611
(800) 545-2433 • fax: (312) 440-9374
e-mail: library@ala.org
Web site: www.ala.org

The ALA is the nation's primary professional organization for librarians. Through its Office for Intellectual Freedom (OIF), the ALA supports free access to libraries and library materials. The OIF also monitors and opposes efforts to ban books. The ALA's sister organization, the Freedom to Read Foundation, provides legal defense for libraries. Publications include the *Newsletter on Intellectual Freedom*, articles, fact sheets, and policy statements, including "Protecting the Freedom to Read."

The Campaign for Press and Broadcasting Freedom (CPBF)

Second Floor., Vi & Garner Smith House, 23 Orford Rd.,
  Walthamstow, London   E17 9NL
020 8521 5932
e-mail: freepress@[NOSPAM]cpbf.org.uk
Web site: www.cpbf.org.uk

The CPBF is an independent organization that lobbies for media reform. Its concerns are ensuring that the media are held accountable for the news they report, rallying against corporate takeovers of the media, and protecting the rights of journalists to cover events without restraint and citizens to redress for imbalanced reporting. The organization publishes media guides, pamphlets, books, and articles, and sponsors conferences on media-related issues.

Columbia Journalism Review (CJR)
Columbia University, Journalism Bldg., 2950 Broadway,
   New York, NY   10027
(212) 854-1881 • fax: (212) 854-8580
e-mail: editors@cjr.org
Web site: www.cjr.org

CJR is a magazine that scrutinizes the performance of the press while examining the political, financial, technological, societal, and legal influences on the media. It is published six times a year under the auspices of Columbia University's Graduate School of Journalism.

Committee to Protect Journalists (CPJ)
330 Seventh Ave., 11th Foorl., New York, NY   10001
(212) 465-1004 • fax: (212) 465-9568
e-mail: info@cpj.org
Web site: www.cpj.org

The CPJ is an independent organization committed to safeguarding press freedom worldwide and upholding the rights of reporters to cover news stories without fear of reprisal. The organization publishes articles that spotlight the mistreatment of journalists and represents the interests of reporters who have been threatened or imprisoned.

Electronic Frontier Foundation (EFF)
454 Shotwell St., San Francisco, CA   94110-1914
(415) 436-9333 • fax: (415) 436-9993
e-mail: information@eff.org
Web site: www.eff.org

The EFF is a nonprofit, nonpartisan organization that works to protect privacy and freedom of expression in the arena of computers and the Internet. Its missions include supporting litigation that protects First Amendment rights. EFF's Web site publishes an electronic bulletin, *EFFector*.

First Amendment Center

First Amendment Center at Vanderbilt University,
   1207 Eighteenth Ave. S., Nashville, TN   37212
(615) 727-1600 • fax: (615) 727-1319
e-mail: info@fac.org
Web site: www.firstamendmentcenter.org

The First Amendment Center emphasizes a range of issues related to the First Amendment. It offers research materials on press freedom (as well as freedom of speech, religion, liberty, assembly, and petition) and circulates First Amendment–related news reports and opinion pieces by legal scholars. The center is operated by the First Amendment Center at Vanderbilt University.

The Freedom Forum

1101 Wilson Blvd., Arlington, VA   22209
(703) 284-2814 • fax: (703) 284-3529
e-mail: news@freedomforum.org,
Web site: www.freedomforum.org

The Freedom Forum is an international organization that works to protect freedom of the press and free speech. It monitors developments in media and First Amendment issues on its Web site, which includes a link to the foundation's "Newseum"—an "interactive museum of news."

The Heritage Foundation

214 Massachusetts Ave. NE, Washington, DC   20002-4999
(202) 546-4400 • fax: (202) 546-8328
e-mail: info@heritage.org
Web site: www.heritage.org

The Heritage Foundation is a conservative public policy institute dedicated to the principles of free competitive enterprise, limited government, individual liberty, and a strong national defense. It believes national security concerns justify limiting the media. The foundation publishes books and research papers by conservative public policy experts.

International Freedom of Expression Exchange (IFEX)
The IFEX Clearing House, 555 Richmond St. W.,
   PO Box #407, Toronto, ON M5V 3B1
(416) 515-9622 • fax: (416) 515-7879
e-mail: ifex@ifex.org
Web site: www.ifex.org

IFEX consists of more than forty organizations that support freedom of expression. Its work is coordinated by its Toronto-based clearinghouse, managed by Canadian Journalists for Free Expression. Organizations report abuses of free expression to the clearinghouse, which circulates that information throughout the world. IFEX distributes the *Communiqué*, an e-mail publication that reports on free expression triumphs and violations.

International Press Institute (IPI)
Spiegelgasse 2, Vienna A-1010
   Austria
(+ 43 1) 512 90 11 • fax: (+ 43 1) 512 90 14
e-mail: ipi@freemedia.at
Web site: www.freemedia.at/wpfr/world_m.htm

The IPI is an international organization of journalists, editors, and media executives who are committed to press freedom and the betterment of the practice of journalism. It fosters communication between media professionals across the globe by publishing articles on and overviews of the state of journalism.

John S. and James L. Knight Foundation
Wachovia Financial Center, Suite 3300, 200 S. Biscayne Blvd.,
Miami, FL 33131-2349
(305) 908-2600

e-mail: web@knightfdn.org
Web site: www.knightfdn.org/default.asp

The foundation is a private, independent organization that advocates for the protection and preservation of press freedom in the United States and abroad. It circulates information related to free press issues and offers grants to journalism-related organizations.

National Coalition Against Censorship (NCAC)
275 Seventh Ave., New York, NY   10001
(212) 807-6222 • fax: (212) 807-6245
e-mail: ncac@ncac.org
Web site: www.ncac.org

The NCAC is an alliance of fifty national nonprofit organizations that works to prevent suppression of free speech and the press. The organization educates the public about the dangers of censorship and how to oppose it. It publishes the newsletter *Censorship News* four times a year, along with articles, reports, and background papers.

People for the American Way (PFAW)
2000 M St. NW, Suite 400, Washington, DC   20036
(202) 467-4999 or (800) 326-PFAW • fax: (202) 293-2672
e-mail: pfaw@pfaw.org
Web site: www.pfaw.org/pfaw/general

PFAW works to promote citizen participation in democracy and safeguard the principles of the U.S. Constitution, including freedom of expression. It distributes educational materials, leaflets, and brochures and publishes the annual *Attacks on the Freedom to Learn*.

Student Press Law Center
1101 Wilson Blvd., Suite 1100, Arlington, VA   22209
(703) 807-1904
e-mail: admin@splc.org
Web site: www.splc.org

The SPLC supports the rights of student journalists and offers information, guidance, and legal aid free of charge to students and their instructors. The organization disseminates information related to legal and censorship issues. Its publications include *Law of the Student Press* and the magazine *SPLC Report*. The SPLC shares office space with the Reporters Committee for Freedom of the Press, which provides free legal assistance to professional journalists.

World Association of Newspapers (WAN)
7 Rue Geoffroy, St. Hilaire, Paris   75005
 France
(33-1) 47 42 85 00 • fax: (33-1) 47 42 49 48
e-mail: contact_us@wan.asso.fr
Web site: www.wan-press.org

WAN is an international organization of newspaper associations and media executives representing over one hundred countries. It promotes and defends press freedom globally, stressing that the fiscal independence of newspapers is a vital requirement to ensure that freedom. WAN contests press controls and campaigns against violations of press freedom.

World Press Freedom Committee (WPFC)
11690-C Sunrise Valley Dr., Reston, VA   20191
(703) 715-9811 • fax: (703) 620-6790
e-mail: freepress@wpfc.org
Web site: www.wpfc.org

The WPFC is an international umbrella organization concerned with freedom of the press on a global level. Its activities include monitoring free press issues, speaking out against those who would rebuff truth in journalism, and granting legal support to journalists put on trial by governments.

For Further Research

Books

Randall P. Bezanson, *How Free Can the Press Be?* Urbana: University of Illinois Press, 2003.

Nancy C. Cornwell, *Freedom of the Press: Rights and Liberties Under the Law*. Santa Barbara, CA: ABC-CLIO, 2004.

Richard C. Cortner, *The Kingfish and the Constitution: Huey Long, the First Amendment, and the Emergence of Modern Press Freedom in America*. Westport, CT: Greenwood, 1996.

Daniel Ellsberg, *Secrets: A Memoir of Vietnam and the Pentagon Papers*. New York: Viking, 2002.

Fred W. Friendly, *Minnesota Rag*. New York: Random House, 1981.

Robin Gerber, *Katharine Graham: The Leadership Journey of an American Icon*. New York: Portfolio, 2005.

Morton J. Horwitz, *The Warren Court and the Pursuit of Justice*. New York: Hill & Wang, 1998.

Dennis J. Hutchinson, *The Man Who Once Was Whizzer White: A Portrait of Justice Byron R. White*. New York: Free Press, 1998.

Harry Kalven Jr., *A Worthy Tradition: Freedom of Speech in America*. New York: Harper and Row, 1988.

Anthony Lewis, *Make No Law: The Sullivan Case and the First Amendment*. New York: Random House, 1991.

Tony Mauro, *Illustrated Great Decisions of the Supreme Court*. Washington, D.C.: CQ, 2000.

Frank I. Michelman, *Brennan and Democracy*. Princeton, NJ: Princeton University Press, 1999.

Lucas A. Powe Jr., *The Fourth Estate and the Constitution: Freedom of the Press in America*. Berkeley: University of California Press, 1991.

John Prados and Margaret Pratt Porter, eds., *Inside the Pentagon Papers*. Lawrence: University Press of Kansas, 2004.

Norman L. Rosenberg, *Protecting the Best Men: An Interpretive History of the Law of Libel*. Chapel Hill: University of North Carolina Press, 1986.

David Rudenstine, *The Day the Presses Stopped: A History of the Pentagon Papers Case*. Berkeley: University of California Press, 1996.

Richard Norton Smith, *The Colonel: The Life and Legend of Robert R. McCormick*. Boston: Houghton Mifflin, 1997.

Rodney A. Smolla, *Suing the Press*. New York: Oxford University Press, 1986.

Geoffrey R. Stone, *Perilous Times: Free Speech in Wartime from the Sedition Act of 1798 to the War on Terrorism*. New York: W.W. Norton, 2004.

Sandra F. Van Burkleo, Kermit L. Hall, and Robert J. Kaczorowski, eds., *Constitutionalism and American Culture: Writing the New Constitutional History*. Lawrence: University Press of Kansas, 2002.

Francis Wilkinson, *Essential Liberty: First Amendment Battles for a Free Press*. New York: Columbia University Graduate School of Journalism, 1992.

Marda Liggett Woodbury, *Stopping the Presses: The Murder of Walter W. Liggett*. Minneapolis: University of Minnesota Press, 1998.

Periodicals

General Articles on Freedom of the Press and the First Amendment

Alan Barth, "Perspective: Course by Newspaper: The Guardian of a Free Society," *Chicago Tribune*, December 6, 1975.

James Boylan, "Punishing the Press: The Public Passes Some Tough Judgements on Libel, Fairness, and 'Fraud,'" *Columbia Journalism Review*, March/April 1997.

Chicago Tribune, "The Free American Press," July 4, 1976.

Ronald K. L. Collins et al., "Speech & Power: Is First Amendment Absolutism Obsolete?" *Nation*, July 21, 1997.

Christopher R. Edgar, "The Right to Freedom of Expressive Association and the Press," *Stanford Law Review*, October 2002.

Dennis Hale, "State Supreme Court Justices' Views on Free Expression," *Newspaper Research Journal*, Winter 2001.

Neil Hickey, "How They Can Help Us, How They Can Hurt Us," *Columbia Journalism Review*, September 2000.

Near v. Minnesota (1931)

Robert Corn-Revere, "The Feds vs. Obscenity: Putting the First Out of Business," *Nation*, September 26, 1988.

Fred W. Friendly, "A 45-Year-Old Rivet in the First Amendment," *New York Times*, June 9, 1976.

John P. MacKenzie, "Prior Restraint Action May Be a Precedent," *Washington Post*, June 16, 1971.

New York Times v. Sullivan (1964)

Floyd Abrams, "Why We Should Change the Libel Law," *New York Times*, September 29, 1985.

Harold Evans, "Beyond the Scoop," *New Yorker*, July 8, 1996.

Jonathan Friendly, "Does a 'Public Figure' Have a Right to Privacy? Well . . . ," *New York Times*, June 12, 1983.

Martin Garbus, "So Nu? So Sue Me," *Nation*, June 7, 1993.

Fred D. Gray, "The Sullivan Case: A Direct Product of the Civil Rights Movement," *Case Western Reserve Law Review*, Fall 1992.

Anthony Lewis, "A Widening Freedom," *New York Times*, October 21, 1994.

Newsweek, "Absence of Malice," February 2, 1985.

Jeffrey Rosen, "The End of Obscenity," *New Republic*, July 15, 1996.

Wendy Tannenbaum, "'Actual Malice' and Product Disparagement," *News Media & the Law*, Summer 2003.

Austin C. Wehrwein, "The News Business: Can the Press Police Itself?" *Washington Post*, March 14, 1972.

New York Times Company v. United States (the Pentagon Papers case) (1971)

R.W. Apple Jr., "Lessons from the Pentagon Papers," *New York Times*, June 23, 1996.

Dorothy Giobbe, "Pentagon Papers' Strategist," *Editor & Publisher*, January 27, 1996.

Fred P. Graham, "U.S. v. Press: Landmark Case on Great Issue of 'Prior Restraint,'" *New York Times*, June 27, 1971.

Morton H. Halperin, "Never Question the President," *Nation*, September 29, 1984.

Kathiann M. Kowalski, "Protecting Freedom of the Press from Presidential Censorship," *Cobblestone*, January 2003.

Anthony Lewis, "When Truth Is Treason," *New York Times*, June 9, 2001.

Richard A. Moore, "The Court Didn't Say It Was Against the Law," *Washington Post*, July 23, 1983.

David Rudenstine, "Pentagon Papers, 20 Years Later," *New York Times*, June 30, 1991.

Branzburg v. Hayes (1972)

Mark Bowden, "Lowering My Shield: A Murder Case, a Subpoena, and a Reporter Ready to Go to Jail to Protect What He Knows. Why Did He Start to Feel Like a Dope?" *Columbia Journalism Review*, July/August 2004.

Monica Dias, "Branzburg Revisited," *News Media and the Law*, March 31, 2002.

Geri L. Dreiling, "Threats of Jail: Is Journalism's 'Fragile Privilege' at Risk? Reporters Face Growing Legal Pressures to Reveal Sources," *National Catholic Reporter*, December 17, 2004.

Anthony L. Fargo, "Is Protection from Subpoenas Slipping? An Analysis of Three Recent Cases Involving Broadcast News Outtakes," *Journal of Broadcasting & Electronic Media*, September 2003.

Annette Fuentes, "The Subpoena Club: Survey of News Organizations by Reporters Committee for Freedom of the Press," *Columbia Journalism Review*, March/May 1992.

Bennett L. Gershman, "Despite Outcry, Abuse Rare," *National Law Journal*, January 10, 2005.

Peter Johnson, "Should Reporters Give Up a Confidential Source?" *USA Today*, August 25, 2004.

Jane E. Kirtley, "Newsgathering Is the New Target," *Columbia Journalism Review*, September 2000.

Carol Marin, "Press Needs Shield Now More than Ever," *Chicago Sun-Times*, November 2, 2005.

Laura Merritt, "Questionable Procedure: Deciding Who Should Be Covered by a Federal Shield Law," *Quill*, October/November 2005.

Jack Nelson, "Newsmen Must Answer Queries of Grand Juries, Court Decides," *Los Angeles Times*, June 30, 1972.

Rik Scarce, "Confidential Sources," *Progressive*, October 1993.

Benjamin Wittes, "Leaks and the Law: What Happens When the Journalistic Principle of Protecting Confidential Sources Clashes with the Public Interest in Prosecuting a Crime? A Cross-Examination," *Atlantic Monthly*, December 2004.

Allan Wolper, "Miller's Handing Over Notes Was Her Major Misstep," *Editor & Publisher*, November 5, 2005.

Web Sites

FindLaw (www.findlaw.com). Features an array of U.S. Supreme Court–related information, including an archive of Court opinions.

The Legal Information Institute (www.law.cornell.edu). Sponsored by Cornell University Law School, features a wealth of legal information, including Supreme Court decisions.

The Oyez Project (www.oyez.org). Sponsored by Northwestern University, features audio files of over two thousand hours of U.S. Supreme Court oral arguments, dating to the 1950s.

U.S. Supreme Court (www.supremecourtus.gov). Features a wide array of Court-related information.

Willamette Law Online (www.willamette.edu). Features summaries of the most recent Supreme Court cases.

Index